This is a work of fiction. All the characters and events portrayed in this novel are fictitious or used fictitiously. All rights reserved. No part of this book may be reproduced in any form or by any electronic or mechanical means, including information storage and retrieval systems, without written permission from the publisher or author, except in the case of a reviewer, who may quote brief passages in a review.

:CBC
\MAZON
゙ /2016

Forever and Always

Book Two of the Forever and Always series

E. L. Todd

For Cindy and Doug,

My second parents and my close friends. You always believed in me and made me feel special. Thank you for allowing me to be a third daughter to your warm family.

"But it was not your fault but mine

And it was your heart on the line

I really fucked it up this time

Didn't I, my dear?

Didn't I, my dear?"

"Little Lion Man" –Mumford and Sons

1

Sean's arms were wrapped around me. The smell of his skin and the feel of his body against mine were almost unreal. I had never been so happy in my life. I almost didn't believe it. Sean was mine. He came all the way to Seattle just to prove his love for me. It was so unexpected and so joyous that I thought my heart would explode. I didn't care about the past anymore. As long as Sean was with me nothing else mattered. My greatest friend was my lover. There was no misunderstanding. Sean loved me. Me.

Sean pulled away from me and approached the table. "Hey," he said to Ryan. They shook hands. "Is it cool if I date your sister?"

Ryan laughed. "Are you asking for my permission?"

"It's just a formality."

"Welcome to the family."

I wrapped my arm around Sean and he held my hand in his own. Sean turned to Cortland. "I'm Sean," he said. "It's nice to meet you."

Cortland nodded. "I'm Cortland. And the pleasure is all mine."

Cortland and I shared a glance and I knew what he meant. Was I going to tell Sean about us? Since Sean and I weren't together or even speaking when it happened, I didn't see the relevance. It was none of his business.

"Now we have a double date." I smiled at Cortland.

"Yes," he said. "We do."

Sean turned to me. "I've never been to Seattle before. Do you want to show me around?"

"I would love to," I said as I kissed him.

"You're welcome to stay with us," Ryan said.

"I would hope so." I smiled. "Since I'm paying the rent and feeding you."

Ryan sighed. "There goes my sister again—being a brat."

Sean nodded. "If you don't mind," he said to my brother.

"Not in the least," Ryan replied. "How long are you staying?"

"Just for the weekend," he said. "Then I'll take Scarlet back home on Sunday."

"What do you mean?" I asked.

"We are going back to New York," he said.

I thought for a moment. This was a complication I hadn't considered. New York used to be my home but it was no longer—Seattle was. I looked at Ryan, but he didn't meet my gaze. This was something he already anticipated and he seemed to be fine with it—on the surface.

"I don't have an apartment or a job, Sean," I said.

"You can live with me," he said. "We'll be together all the time anyway."

"I don't know," I said apprehensively.

"What do you mean?"

"You should go, Scarlet," Ryan said. "New York is your home."

I met my brother's gaze and he was smiling at me, giving me his permission to leave. The idea of being away from him again made my heart ache. We had reconnected in such a strong way, and I didn't want to lose that, but I couldn't make Sean leave his job in New York. I wasn't even sure where he would work in Seattle.

"We'll discuss it later," I said to Sean.

Sean stared at me for a moment, but didn't say anything.

"Let's drop off your stuff at the apartment and I'll show you around." I smiled.

"Okay," he said.

"We'll see you later," I said to the two men. Cortland nodded and Ryan waved. Sean and I walked out the door and headed up the street, hand in hand, as we watched the Seattle lights in the nighttime air.

"It's beautiful here," he said.

"I know."

"Do you like it here?" he asked. "I know this is where you grew up."

"I do."

"So, what are we doing about New York?" he asked as we approached the apartment building. "I need to buy your ticket before they are sold out."

I sighed. "I don't know, Sean."

"What do you mean?"

We walked through the lobby and stood in the elevator, rising up to the fifth floor. Sean squeezed my hand as we left the elevator and made it to the door. "I'm not going anywhere, Scarlet. You are the one for me. Please don't be scared."

I smiled at him. "That's not what I was thinking." I inserted the key in the lock and opened the door. Sean walked inside and put his bag in the living room then looked around the apartment. He turned his gaze back to me and I reveled in how handsome he was. Somehow I had forgotten. Suddenly, I realized I was wearing gym clothes because Ryan and I played basketball for an hour. Sean seemed to read my mind.

"You are so beautiful," he said. "I don't know how I didn't notice it before."

My cheeks blushed from his comment. I was wearing a baggy sweatshirt and my hair was in a loose braid. I knew I was a mess.

"Tell me why you don't want to come home with me," he said as he stood in front of me. He held my hand in his own and caressed my fingers. "We don't have to live together. I just assumed that we would—I want to. I'm with you all the time anyway."

I smiled at him. "I would love to live with you."

"Then what's the problem?"

"I—I ignored Ryan for the past year and made no effort to

stay in contact with him. When I came back to Seattle, I saw how much that hurt him. He has been spending the holidays with friends—sometimes alone—and now that we're together again, everything is better. I—I don't know if I can leave him again."

Sean sighed. "We will both make an effort to stay in touch with him, Scarlet. I'll remind you to call him every day. And I don't mind spending the holidays with him. He can even come to my family estate in Connecticut—he's my family, too."

"I don't think Ryan would accept that," I whispered. "And it isn't the same. It's impossible to stay close when you're on opposite ends of the country. Without mutual experiences, you run out of things to discuss—you don't connect. My brother is the one who took care of me and got me back on my feet, despite what I did to him. I won't do it again. I can't leave him, Sean."

"Do you feel this way because of guilt or desire?" he asked. "Would you rather stay with him?"

I thought for a moment. "I don't want to leave him."

Sean sighed. "My job is in New York. I can't just leave it. I have no idea if I could even find a job here in Seattle."

"I know," I whispered. "We can do long-distance. We can take turns flying back every weekend."

Sean dropped my hand and stepped back. "Until when?" he asked. "I want to marry you at some point. We are going to have to make a compromise eventually. Ryan can take care of himself—he understands that you have to move on with your life."

His comment about marriage made my heart flutter. "You

want to marry me?"

Sean smiled at me. "I'm sorry if I didn't make that clear," he said. "I want to be with you for always. Does it change anything? Will you move to New York with me?"

"Let me think about it," I said.

"For how long?" he asked sadly.

"A few weeks," I answered.

"So, I won't see you for five days every week?" he asked. "That sounds terrible."

"It'll be okay," I said. "It's temporary. I'll make a decision eventually."

"What other option do we have? You either move to New York or you don't."

"You could come here," I suggested.

"And work where?" he asked.

"We would figure it out," I said. "I could support us until you find something."

Sean sighed. "I appreciate that, but I will never let you support me—ever. I refuse to let that happen."

I rolled my eyes. He reminded me of Cortland in that respect.

"I caught that," he said. "I'm sorry I'm being difficult, but I want this to work. I was looking forward to being with you."

"I'm being difficult, too," I said. "Just give me some time. Let Ryan get used to the idea of me leaving."

"So, you are moving then?" he asked happily.

"I—I don't know."

Sean's smiled dropped. "I am willing to do a long-distance relationship—anything—to be with you. But I want to live with you soon. We are going to have to figure it out."

"I understand," I said. "Just give me some time. Maybe there is a way I can still see Ryan periodically."

Sean sighed. "Since I'm the one that fucked this up and drove you away, I'll be patient. This wouldn't be happening if I wasn't such an idiot."

"I forgive you, Sean—let's just forget about it."

"I don't deserve you."

I grabbed his face and kissed him gently and his lips ignited a fire within me. His lips felt right against mine and I knew I was meant for him—we were perfect together. I pulled away from him. "I love you so much," I whispered.

Sean pressed his forehead against mine. "I love you, too, Scar. I'm sorry that I hurt you."

"It doesn't matter anymore," I said.

He rubbed his nose against mine and I felt the stress leave my body. My brother and I were close again and Sean was mine—really *mine*. My editing company was a success and everything was great. The student loan fiasco was still weighing on me, but I pushed it back, wanting to forget about it now that Sean was with me.

"In a way, I'm glad that this happened," I said.

He pulled away from me. "Why?"

"I never would have fixed the relationship between Ryan and I, and I never would have started my own company. A lot of great things have happened because of it."

"I'm glad," he said. "My life has been nothing but miserable without you. I'm grateful that Ryan took care of you."

I held him for a moment, and we stood together in silence. Leaving Ryan was something I wasn't sure I could do. After everything we'd been through, I didn't think I could move away and not see him every day, especially for a guy that hurt me so much. I promised myself I wouldn't hurt Ryan again, and I didn't want to. Hopefully, Sean would just grow frustrated with me and move to Seattle to be with me. I didn't want to ask him to do it because that would be selfish but I really wanted him to do it on his own. He knew how important Ryan was to me—I couldn't leave him.

"So," he said. "Can I take you to dinner?"

"Well, I just ate."

"When has that ever stopped you?" He smiled.

I hit him lightly on the shoulder. We were back to the way we were, except our relationship was different. It seemed like we had the best of both worlds—our friendship and our love. "Stop making fun of me."

"I make fun of you because I love you. Think about it that way."

"That doesn't help." I smiled.

"How about some dessert, then?" he asked.

"Well, I just had a milkshake."

Sean smiled. "Then let me take you out for a drink."

"Are you trying to get me drunk?"

He shrugged. "We'll see what happens."

"I'm going to shower and change," I said. "Please make yourself at home."

"Thank God," Sean said. "I was worried that you were going to go out like that."

I grabbed his stomach and tickled him. "You got me," he laughed. "But you know I think you're beautiful no matter what you wear, even my old college jersey."

"Well, I'm a hot piece of ass," I said as I walked away.

"You are *my* hot piece of ass now."

I turned around and looked at him before I disappeared in the hallway. "I like it."

"Good," he said. "Get used to it."

I showered then changed my clothes, wearing a tight fitting dress that accentuated the curves of my body. After I applied my makeup, I looked in the mirror and felt satisfied. I looked like a million bucks.

When I came back into the living room, Ryan and Cortland were sitting on the couch with Sean, and they all looked at me when I walked into the room. Sean was blatantly staring at me with a hungry expression.

He stood up and walked towards me. "You look—"

"You better get it right this time." I smiled.

Sean smiled at me. "Like a wild, sexy beast."

"Thank you," I said. "That was just the compliment I was looking for."

Sean laughed. "Are you ready to go?"

"Where are you guys going?" Ryan asked.

"Well, since this fatty already ate and stuffed herself with a milkshake, I am taking her out for a drink."

"My sister can be a garbage disposal," Ryan said.

"Now look who's being a brat," I said to my brother.

He laughed then looked at Sean. "Good luck with her."

"Thanks." Sean laughed. "I think I'm going to need it."

"When did this turn into a Scarlet-bashing?" I asked.

Sean kissed me on my head. "It's only because we love you."

I looked at him. "Well, maybe you should try hating me instead."

"Let's go," Sean said. He turned to Ryan. "I'll have her home in a few hours."

"She's your problem now," Ryan said. "The weight is off my shoulders."

I rolled my eyes and Sean wrapped his arm around me as we walked to the street. We took a cab to the main strip. Sean and I arrived at a classy piano bar and we took a seat at a table in the corner. A waitress stopped by and took our drink order. I ordered a glass of wine and Sean ordered a beer.

For a long time, Sean just stared at me from across the table without saying anything. I met his look with a smile, waiting for him to speak.

"I can't believe how beautiful you are," he said. "I don't know how I was so oblivious before."

The waitress returned with our beverages then walked away. "That's because you're an idiot." He smiled at my comment. I sipped my wine as I looked at him. "You aren't bad to look at either."

Sean laughed. "So I tell you how beautiful you are and all I get is, 'you aren't bad to look at?'"

I shrugged. "I think you are the most handsome man I've ever seen."

Sean nodded. "That's better."

"I mean it."

"I know you do."

He drank from his beer while he continued to stare at me. I met his look with a smirk on my lips. I enjoyed the attention he was giving me. Other men I had met often seemed immediately smitten with me, but Sean never was, but now the man was infatuated with me. I loved it. When I walked into the bar, heads immediately turned to look at me and I knew Sean noticed it. A few men were still staring.

Sean noticed the gawking. "Now I'm going to have to deal with people looking at my girlfriend all the time."

I shrugged. "Get used to it."

He laughed. "You aren't conceited at all."

"You are confusing arrogance with confidence."

Sean smiled at me then looked down at his glass. "I'm glad that you are doing so well. Ryan told me how hurt you were when you arrived here. I'm really grateful that he took care of you."

"When did he tell you that?" I asked.

Sean sighed. "I've been calling him to check on you—make sure you were okay."

I stared at him for a moment. "You've been doing that the whole time?"

He nodded. "I would have called you instead, but I knew you didn't want to speak with me—and rightfully so."

"I had no idea."

"I called him the day after you left, wanting to make sure you were with him—somewhere safe. I admit I was hurt that you just took off without saying a word to me. I was ready to apologize for everything after I cooled off for a day, but you were already on the other side of the country."

I felt horrible. "I'm sorry, Sean."

"It's not your fault," he said. "I understood why you left. I was the one who messed everything up."

"Please don't blame yourself. In the end, if that hadn't happened, we wouldn't be together now. I guess it was the greatest thing that ever happened to us—for me, at least."

Sean rested his hand on top of mine. "This is the best thing that has ever happened to me too."

I immediately thought of Penelope, but I didn't want to ask

him about her. They hadn't been broken up very long, so it was unrealistic that he would be completely over her, but I didn't want to hear him say it. I decided to leave it alone. He would forget about her eventually, and I didn't want to wait anyway. We were both happiest when we were together.

"When did you know?" I asked.

A man in a suit approached a piano on the stage and began to play softly. The light music echoed around the room. The tables were filled with couples talking privately, and the dim lighting of the bar made everyone feel relaxed.

Sean met my gaze. "I don't know," he said. "I think I've always known. Even before you left, I started to realize how much I needed you—always. When we were apart, I thought about you constantly and realized how much I missed you. It was the morning after you left that I went to your apartment to try to work things out. I wanted to be with you then, but when I found that you were already gone, I knew how much I'd hurt you. Ryan and I thought it was best if I left you alone."

I nodded. "That makes sense. I was in a really dark place, but Ryan helped me out of it. I think I'm a stronger person from the experience."

"I can tell," he said.

"How are things at work?" I asked as I drank from my wine.

"It's fine," he said.

"Did you play racquetball with your boss?"

"No." Sean laughed. "After he realized you weren't coming, he called it off and started to ignore me at work."

"That's ridiculous."

Sean nodded. "There is a fine line between sex and politics."

"Was he actually expecting to sleep with me?" I asked. "That's disturbing."

"No. He just likes to be around pretty women. It makes him look better—more powerful."

"Men," I said in a disgusted voice. "And I can't believe you tried to set me up with one."

"Brian isn't like that," he said. "He just acts weird around you."

"Are you going to tell him that I'm your girlfriend?"

He nodded. "I'm going to tell anyone who will listen—*twice.*"

I laughed and almost spilled my wine. "You're sweet."

"Only for you," he said.

The memory of him sleeping with Janice came back to my mind, along with the hurt and the betrayal. I wondered if he continued to sleep with her after I left, but I decided not to ask.

"Have you talked to Janice?" I asked.

Sean looked uncomfortable at the mention of her. "Yes," he said. "She's really worried about you. She wanted me to tell you that she's sorry and that she loves you. You are still her best friend."

I nodded. "Maybe I should call her."

"You should," Sean said. "I know you're mad at her, but she feels horrible about what happened. In her defense, you lied to her about your feelings for me. I think you should give her a chance."

I sighed. "I think you're right."

"Thank you," he said. "And Scarlet, I want you to know that I didn't sleep with anyone when we were apart—that includes Janice."

The news made me happy, but I tried to hide my glee. It was obvious how much he loved me by staying faithful to me even though we weren't together. Guilt flooded my mind when I thought about Cortland. I didn't know if I should tell him. I didn't respond to his words and Sean didn't ask me if I had slept with anyone, thankfully. I wasn't sure what my answer would have been.

"Are you ready to go?" he asked. "It's almost midnight—three in New York."

"Sure," I said. "You must be tired."

Sean dropped the money on the table and we left, taking a taxi back to the apartment. Sean wrapped his arm around my shoulder and I placed my hand on his thigh. We were really a couple and it felt right—perfect.

When we got back to the apartment, Ryan was already in his room sleeping. I walked towards my bedroom, but Sean moved into the living room.

"What are you doing?" I asked.

"Getting ready for bed," he said.

"You're coming into my room with me," I said. "You aren't sleeping on the couch."

"I don't mind," he said.

I walked over to him and grabbed his hand. "Don't be annoying, Sean. Come to bed with me."

Sean didn't move. "Scarlet, I don't think I should." I sat down beside him and rested my hand on top of his.

"Why not?" I asked.

Sean sighed. "I know if I sleep next to you, I'm going to make a move."

"I want you to." I smiled.

"I want to take this slow," he said. "I don't want to mess this up again. Besides, your brother is in the next room."

I rolled my eyes. "He's had girls over before. And we've already slept together, Sean. I really want to do it again." I ran my hand up his thigh and he closed his eyes.

Sean stopped my hand. "I love you, Scarlet, and I respect you. I'm willing to wait until you're ready."

"I am *ready*, Sean."

"Let's give it some time."

"Are you afraid to be with me?" I asked sadly.

He shook his head. "Absolutely not," he said quickly. "Believe me, I want you, Scarlet. Seeing you wearing that dress tonight made me want to take you in the middle of that bar, but I can't rush this because I love you. I don't want to jump into something you aren't ready for, even if you say you are. I know how much I hurt you, and I want make sure that you trust me before we begin a physical relationship."

"I do trust you, Sean. Stop being a prude."

Sean laughed. "You have no idea how much I don't want to be," he said. "I've thought about making love to you since the first time I had you. You never told me you were amazing in bed."

"Well, it never came up." I smiled.

Sean kissed my forehead. "Don't doubt my desire for you. I just want to treat you right."

I sighed. "Fine," I said.

Sean smiled at me. "I love that you want me so much."

"Well, you know your way around the bedroom, too. And I love you, Sean. I want to make love to the man I'm in love with."

"You'll get your chance," he said as he patted my thigh.

"Can I at least kiss you?"

"If you can control yourself." He smiled.

"Look who's conceited now," I said.

Sean grabbed my face and kissed me, moving my lips slowly with his own. His fingers glided through my hair as he parted my lips with his tongue, and I felt myself gasp involuntarily. I forgot how great of a kisser he was. My hands were running through his hair by their own will. Sean laid me back on the couch, spreading my legs with his hips. He glided his hand down my legs and massaged my calf then moved his hands back to my face. My fingers scratched his back as we kissed on the couch. I wanted more, but I knew he would never give it to me. Sean didn't touch my breasts or the area between my legs as he caressed the rest of my body. Finally, he broke our kiss and stared at me.

"You should go to bed. I don't know if I can be a gentleman any longer."

"I don't want you to be."

He pressed his forehead against mine and sighed. "Please don't say that to me."

"Sean, I want you."

He growled and moved away from me. "Good night, Scar," he said.

I pulled down my dress and got to my feet. "I'll grab you some blankets," I said as I walked to the closet. I tossed him a sheet and an extra pillow then stood in front of him.

"Thank you," he said.

I pushed him back and sat on his lap, straddling his hips.

"It isn't going to work," he whispered.

I sighed, annoyed that I wasn't going to get any. I kissed him gently. "I love you."

"I love you too," he said as he cupped my face.

"Good night," I said as I got to my feet.

"Good night, babe."

I smiled at him. "*Babe*?"

"What?"

"Why are you calling me that?"

"You're my girlfriend—I can call you whatever I want."

I turned around and walked toward the hallway. "I'll see you in the morning."

"Good night," he said.

2

When I woke up the next morning, Sean was still asleep on the couch. Instead of walking into the living room in my pajamas with no makeup, I dolled myself up for my new boyfriend, not wanting him to see me look so hideous. I had never been happier in my life, and even though I really wanted to sleep with Sean, knowing he was in the next room was enough.

I sat at the kitchen table and ate my cereal quietly, letting Sean sleep as long as possible since he was still acclimating to the time difference. Ryan came in a moment later and spotted Sean on the couch. He poured himself a cup of coffee and sat across from me, reading the newspaper like he did every morning. Ryan didn't strike me as a guy that cared about local news in Seattle, but he read the paper every single day.

I heard a loud yawn from the living room and knew Sean was awake. He got up and stretched, and I walked over to him, giving him a kiss.

"Good morning," I said.

"Good morning." He smiled. "Sorry I slept in so late."

"I'm glad you got some rest," I said. "Would you like some breakfast?"

"I'll just have coffee." Sean rose from the couch and entered the kitchen, pouring himself a mug of coffee. He sat at the table with us while I had breakfast. I was practically jumping in my seat because I was so happy. Ryan smiled at me from across the table.

"I'm surprised you slept on the couch," Ryan said.

"I didn't mind," Sean said quickly.

"I would have given you my bed," Ryan said. "Guests should never sleep on the couch."

"Thank you," he said. "But the couch is fine, really."

"I offered to let him sleep with me, but he refused," I said.

Ryan shook his head. "That's because Sean has some class—unlike you."

I rolled my eyes at my brother.

Ryan turned the page of the newspaper. "Do you want to play ball with Cortland and I?" he asked. "We are leaving in a few minutes."

"Sure," Sean said before I could reject the offer. Now that Sean was there and only for a weekend, I wanted to spend all my time with him. "Do you have some clothes I can borrow?"

"Yeah," Ryan said.

Cortland knocked on the door just then. "Come in," Ryan said.

Cortland came into the kitchen with the basketball in his hands. He smiled to me then nodded at Sean. "You guys coming?"

"Yeah," Sean said. "We can play teams."

"Yay," I said sarcastically.

Sean smiled at me. "I am yours for the rest of the day."

"You better be."

"I'm going to change," Sean said as he got up.

"I'll grab you some clothes," Ryan said as he followed him.

Cortland sat down next to me. "Did you tell him?"

"No." I sighed. "And I don't think I'm going to."

"Don't you think he has the right to know?"

"Well, we weren't together—or even speaking—at the time. I don't think it's any of his business. Besides, it will just make it awkward between you two, and since nothing is ever going to happen between us again, he has no reason to feel threatened by you. I think it's best if we don't tell him."

"Well, Ryan might."

I shook my head. "No, he won't."

"So, if he asks if you slept with anyone, you're just going to lie?"

"No," I said quickly. "I'll make up a fictitious person."

"If you think that's best." He sighed.

"I do," I said. "I don't want to ruin my friendship with you. And that's all we are—friends."

Cortland shrugged. "It's up to you."

Ryan and Sean came back and we left the apartment, walking to the courts a few blocks away. Sean held my hand as we walked, and when we got to the basketball court, we started a game of two on two.

"I pick Cortland," Ryan said quickly. "I'm not going to be on my sister's team—she sucks."

"Damn." Sean sighed. "Now I'm stuck with her."

I hit him lightly on the shoulder, and he laughed at me. "You don't want me on your team?"

He wrapped his arms around me. "Not if I want to win."

"Come on, lovebirds. Let's play," Ryan shouted.

I narrowed my eyes at him. "Well, what's more important to you? Winning this game or having a girlfriend?" I asked.

Sean stroked his chin like he was deep in thought, and I hit him again. "Okay," he said quickly. "I'm happy that I'm on your team."

"Good." I smiled. "That's better."

We started the game, but I lagged behind the three men. Sean tried to keep me involved by stealing the ball from Ryan then tossing it to me. Then he would block the men from moving towards me so I could make a shot. The rest of the game went that way. Of course, we lost, but we had a lot of fun playing it. Sean and I were both sweaty when the game ended, so he grabbed my shirt and wiped his forehead on it.

"You're so gross," I yelled as I pulled my shirt away.

He grabbed my face and kissed me. "You are too," he said as he licked his lips. "But I like it, so it's okay."

"Mega-Shake?" Ryan asked.

"Let's do it," Cortland said.

We walked to the shop and ordered our food. We all washed our hands before we took a seat in the corner.

"You guys come here a lot?" Sean asked.

"Yes," I answered. "Ryan and I used to come here almost every day as kids to get shakes."

"Yes, my sister would drag me here constantly," Ryan said.

I threw a fry at my brother. "You wanted to come here more than I did."

Most of the time, my brother and I would stay there and do our homework until we had to go home, wanting to be out of the house as much as possible. My father passed away, leaving us alone with a mother that hated us with every fiber of her being. My mother used to hit me when she was drunk, but Ryan would always intervene and take the beating himself, protecting me with his body. I looked up at Ryan and we shared the same thought. This place was our safe haven.

Ryan finished his food and pushed it away. "Cortland and I are going to a comedy show tonight," he said.

Cortland nodded. "I got free tickets from work," he said. "I would invite you guys, but I only have two tickets."

"What about Monnique?" I asked.

"She has to work," Cortland said sadly.

"When are we going to meet her?" I asked.

"I don't know," he said. "I don't want to scare her off, and meeting you might make her run for the hills."

"You are starting to act like Ryan," I said. "You are spending too much time together."

"No," Cortland said. "I think you are just becoming my annoying sister, too."

24

I looked at Sean. "You see what I have to put up with?"

Sean smiled. "I feel bad for them, too."

I pinched his side gently and tickled him. "I don't want to lose you, too."

He looked at me. "Well, if it makes you feel better, I definitely don't think of you as my sister."

"I would hope not," I said with a laugh.

Sean finished his last fry. "I want to order one of these milkshakes now. See what the big deal is."

"You'll love it," I said excitedly.

Sean stared at me for a moment. "I'm sure that I will."

"I'll go order them," I said as I stood up. Cortland was already on his feet.

"So, three chocolates, and what flavor will you be getting, Sean?" Cortland asked.

"Vanilla," he said.

Cortland walked away to order and pay for the shakes before I could even move. "That guy is such a snob," I said as I sat down again.

"He seems like a nice guy to me," Sean said as he shrugged his shoulders.

"And why did you get vanilla?" I asked him. "That is the lame flavor."

"Well, I didn't want strawberry."

"You could have gotten chocolate."

"But you guys all ordered that," he said. "I wasn't going to conform."

"You are so weird." I sighed.

"You're the one that doesn't share milk products, pours the cereal on top of the milk, and you eat hot dogs off the ground." He laughed.

"Don't get me started on that," Ryan said as he shook his head. "Who doesn't share milk products? How is that any different than other products?"

I shook my head as I thought for a moment. "It's just gross."

Sean stared at me. "You're the weirdo," he said. "Sharing a glass of water is just as disgusting."

I made a gagging face. "But milk is thick and pasteurized—and—it's just nasty."

"Okay," Sean said sarcastically. "Now it totally makes sense."

Cortland walked back to the table with our shakes when Ryan said, "You really ate a hotdog off the ground?"

Cortland stopped and stared at me. "Is that true?"

I felt all their eyes fall on me, judging me for what I did. "Well, yeah, it was still good."

"When was this?" Cortland asked.

"When she was in New York," Sean said. "She dropped it on the ground after the vendor handed it to her, but she ate it anyway."

Ryan stared at Sean. Now he was judging him. "And you

kiss her?"

Sean smiled. "Yeah," he said. "She's gross, but I like it."

Cortland stared at me for a moment, and I knew he was grossed out because he had kissed me too. I couldn't help it. I started laughing at the look of disgust on his face.

Ryan turned to Cortland. "And she doesn't share milk products," he said. "Are you sure you want her to be your sister, too?"

"I don't get it," he said. "Why are milk products different than other stuff?"

Sean laughed. "Apparently it's thicker and pasteurized—whatever the hell that means."

"You guys are all jerks," I said as I sat back in my seat.

Sean leaned forward towards Cortland. "And she has to pour her cereal on top of the milk. She won't eat it if the milk goes on last. She claims that it's too soggy."

Cortland started laughing. "So, let me get this straight. You will eat a nasty hotdog off the ground, but you refuse to eat a bowl of cereal because it's too soggy? And you won't share a milkshake with your boyfriend because of all the bacteria?" Ryan started laughing so hard that he was heaving with breaths, and Sean was wiping the tears from his eyes. "That makes absolutely no fucking sense, Scar."

I couldn't help it; I started laughing at their jokes. My ridiculous habits were amusing, even to me. "You made your point," I said as I stopped laughing. I turned to Sean. "Does this change the way you feel about me?"

Sean kissed my lips then pulled away. "I think I love you more."

Ryan shook his head. "Poor guy," he said. "Has no idea what he's getting himself into."

Sean laughed. "No, but I'm excited to find out." He kissed my forehead then finished his shake. "Well, it was pretty good. You were right about that." Sean grabbed my milkshake and drank out of it before I could stop him. "I guess this one is mine, too."

I stared at the straw for a moment before I brought it to my lips. I pulled it away again and couldn't hide the disdain on my face. All the guys were laughing at me, including Sean, so I closed my eyes and drank out of the straw and put it down. "There," I said triumphantly. "I did it."

"Congratulations," Ryan said sarcastically. "Now you're a normal person."

Sean leaned towards me. "I love that you're weird—if that makes it any better. You aren't some unrealistic fantasy—you are real."

I smiled at him, remembering when I said those words to him. "You got that right."

"Don't let him go, Scar," Cortland said. "Otherwise you'll end up alone."

"Thanks." I laughed.

Sean turned towards my brother. "When is this comedy show?"

"Around seven," he said. "What are your plans for the night?"

I wanted to stay in the apartment, particularly in the bedroom, but I knew Sean wouldn't go for it. Sean turned to me. "How about dinner and then we'll rent a movie—something that couples do."

"Are we going to make out while the movie is on?"

"We are an adult couple—not a high school couple," Sean teased.

I sighed. "Fine," I said. "That sounds good."

"Okay," he said. "That sounds like a date."

3

I took Sean to see the Space Needle then to Pike's Market across town. Sean seemed to be intrigued with everything, but I felt like he was paying more attention to me than anything else.

"So, are all people in Seattle obsessed with golf?" he asked when we were in the Space Needle Gift Shop.

I shook my head. "No," I said. "Or I don't think so, at least."

"Let's go to the music museum," he said excitedly.

I looked at my watch and saw that it was almost six. We had been out all day, and I wanted to lie on the couch with him and cuddle like boring couples do. As long as I was with Sean, I was happy, but I wanted to be alone with him.

"Maybe we should head back and change before dinner," I said.

He looked at me for a moment. "Do you even want to go out?" He smiled.

"No, not really," I admitted.

"We can order in," he said.

"That sounds wonderful." I sighed.

"This doesn't change anything," he said. I knew what he was referring to, that he wouldn't sleep with me.

I rolled my eyes. "I just want to be alone with you," I said.

"I want to hold you and cuddle with you. We can't do that in a public place."

"You're right about that," he said. "And we can make out while we watch a movie—if you really want to."

"Yes, please." I smiled.

"I feel like a horny teenager anyway," he said sarcastically.

"We can change that," I said as I kissed his lips.

"You are the devil, Scarlet," he said as he pulled away. "You are practically trying to rape me while I'm trying to respect you."

"I never said I wanted to be respected."

"Well, get over it because I love you, Scar. You are just going to have to deal with it."

"How long are you going to make me wait?" I asked.

Sean sighed. "I don't know," he said. "Until I think you are ready."

"And how will you know if I am?"

I followed Sean out of a store. He opened a cab door and let me inside first. "I don't know," he said. "I just will."

I crossed my arms over my chest and sighed.

"Don't be mad at me, Scar."

"Too late," I said. "I don't get it, Sean. I love you and you love me. We are together and we are happy. You are a part of my family now and we are perfect together. What are you waiting for? I want to make love, Sean."

Sean glanced at the driver then back at me. "We'll continue

this conversation later," he whispered.

I rolled my eyes then stared straight ahead. He grabbed my hand and held it within his own, but I didn't pull it away. Sean started kissing my neck and I felt my anger ebb away as his lips grazed over my skin. "I love you."

"I love you too," I whispered. I was still mad at him, but I loved hearing him tell me that.

When we got back to the apartment, Ryan could tell that I was mad just by looking at me.

"You guys are fighting already?" he asked incredulously.

"No," I said as I sat on the couch and crossed my arms over my chest.

"I've known you your whole life, Scar. I know when you are pissed about something. I suggest you let it go and cut Sean some slack."

"Shut up, Ryan," I snapped.

"I knew I was right." He smiled.

"She's mad that I won't have sex with her," Sean said.

I slapped Sean on the arm. "I can't believe you told him that."

"Well, now you know how ridiculous you sound." He laughed. "I know you tell your brother everything, so what's the big deal?"

"Yes," I snapped. "*I* tell him everything because he's *my* brother. You had no right to tell him that."

"Too late," Sean said.

Ryan laughed. "You are getting mad at your boyfriend for respecting you? Wow, what an asshole," he said sarcastically.

"This doesn't concern you, Ryan," I said.

"Whatever," he said. "You're just going to tell me about it anyway."

I sighed and looked away from the two men. I didn't have any reason to be mad at Ryan, but I was. And I was furious with Sean. Ryan walked down the hall and went into his room to get ready for his evening out. Sean placed his hand on my thigh.

"I'm sorry," he whispered. "You are just making this really difficult for me. You are absolutely gorgeous and sexy, and you have no idea how much I want to be with you, but more importantly, I love you and I want to make sure that I'm not hurting you."

His words softened my anger. I turned towards him and met his gaze. "I've moved on from what happened, Sean. I forgive you, so let's forget about it and be happy together. I trust you and know you will never hurt me again. It was a huge misunderstanding anyway. And I won't let you hurt me again. Last time I thought I couldn't go on, but I'll never allow myself to feel that way again. So please, stop babying me."

Sean sighed. "I'll think about it," he said.

I rolled my eyes. I was done talking about it. "What do you want for dinner?"

Sean thought for a moment. "Chinese food sounds good. Or even pizza."

"Let's do pizza," I said. "We have to find a movie to watch."

"There's probably something on television," he said. "That way we don't have to go out again."

"Okay."

Ryan came back into the living room and grabbed his keys. "I'm leaving," he said as he walked to the door. "It's nice having Sean here so I can go out."

"I never asked you to stay and babysit me," I snapped.

Ryan shrugged. "I'll see you later." He shut the door behind him and was gone.

I rose from the couch and opened up the phone book, looking for a pizza parlor close by. Sean came up behind me and ran his fingers down my back. "Have you called Janice?"

"No." I sighed. "I'll call her when you leave."

"Okay," he said. "I know she'll appreciate it."

"I know."

He kissed me on the cheek then stepped away. "What kind are you going to order?" he asked.

"Combination."

"Are you going to ask them to drop it on the ground before they bring it over?" He smiled.

I picked up the phone and dialed. "You're lucky that I love you."

"The luckiest guy in the world."

The phone started to ring and they finally answered. I

placed our order and hung up. Sean pulled out twenty dollars and left it on the table. "They can keep the change."

"I got it," I said. "You paid for drinks the other night."

"Don't worry about it," he said quickly. "You can get the next one."

His quick refusal made me suspicious. I knew he had been conversing with Ryan, and I wondered if my brother had told him about my situation. I wanted to ask him without giving the information away just in case Ryan hadn't told him.

"I'm making good money from my editing company," I said. "A woman just paid me two thousand dollars to edit her manuscript."

Sean nodded. "I'm going to quit my job and start editing too, then."

"You don't need to pay for everything, Sean. I have money."

"I know," he said. "But you are my girlfriend and I like to treat you. Is it that big of a deal?"

I realized that he didn't know. After all, if he had, he would have said something already. He probably would have yelled at me for not telling him about it to begin with, and berate me for giving all my money to my brother. "No."

"Good," he said. "This feminism movement is annoying. A guy can't even take out a girl anymore."

I smiled. "I didn't mean to offend you, babe."

Sean wrapped me in his arms and nuzzled my neck. "I like

it when you call me that."

"You do?"

"Definitely."

"I like that it isn't weird that we're a couple."

"Me too," he said. "It makes me wonder why we didn't do this sooner."

"That's because you were busy being oblivious to my charms," I teased him.

He pulled away from me. "No," he said. "I know you've always been a hot piece of ass."

I smiled. "And you haven't always been bad to look at."

Sean laughed. "I prefer the other compliment."

"Too bad," I said. There was a knock on the door and I answered it. I handed the man Sean's money and brought the pizza into the living room. Sean and I ate it out of the box like always, and we watched television for a while.

"There are no games on." Sean sighed.

I leaned into him and rested my head on his shoulder, cuddling with him like I've wanted to since he arrived. The scent of his body was evident in my nostrils, and he smelled like home. It reminded me of his apartment. Sean turned off the television and lay down beside me on the couch. His fingers ran through my hair and we stared at each other for a while, just treasuring the fact that we were really together.

"I'm sorry about everything, Scarlet," he whispered. "I hope you believe that."

"I do." I smiled. "And I'm sorry, too."

Sean leaned in and kissed me gently. My senses ignited when we touched. The chemistry between us was powerful and amazing. All the times when Janice accused me of loving Sean, I rejected the idea, refusing to think I could ever love him, but I did, and now it seemed so obvious. If only we hadn't been established as friends first, perhaps we would have been together. Maybe we'd even be married. I cupped his cheek and pulled his lips closer to mine. I slipped my tongue into his mouth, making his body shake. Sean ran his hands down my body and slid one inside my shirt, feeling the skin of my stomach and ribs. My hands reached under his shirt to caress the muscles of his stomach and chest. Just the touch alone sent me over the edge and I knew I wanted him. Why did we have to wait? I climbed on top of Sean and kissed him with more passion. He responded immediately, and I grabbed his hand and placed it over my breast. Sean squeezed it gently then unclasped my bra, letting it fall loose. Sean rolled on top of me then rubbed his nose against mine, making me weak as he looked at me.

"Are you sure?" he whispered. "I want this to be right."

"I love you, Sean," I said. "I want to be with you. And I know that you love me. We are meant for each other." My hands combed through his hair as his eyes drifted shut.

"I love you, Scar," he said as he kissed me.

"I love you."

Sean gathered me in his arms then carried me into my

bedroom, laying me gently on the bed. His shirt felt soft in my fingertips as it slid from his body and dropped to the floor. His strong chest made me feel safe and protected, like he could always defend me. That fueled my arousal even more, knowing that he would never hurt me again. With steady hands, I unbuttoned his pants and pulled them down with his undershorts. He was completely naked on top of me. I kissed his body everywhere, praising his beautiful physique with my mouth. Sean moaned as he watched me for a moment then pulled my shirt from my body and dropped it on the bed. He kissed my chest gently then moved to my neck, trailing kisses down to my stomach. His fingers unbuttoned my pants and he pulled them free, leaving me only in my thong. Sean crawled on top of me and pressed his forehead against mine.

"We can stop," he said.

"Sean, you are being annoying," I said as I grabbed his cock and squeezed it gently.

"I love you," he whispered.

"I love you too, Sean."

"I want this to be perfect for you." He breathed deeply, inhaling my scent.

"It is," I said. "As long as it's with you." His lips were on mine and I kissed him gently. Sean pulled down my underwear and freed me from the material.

"You are gorgeous," he said as he separated my legs with his own.

"I want you," I said as he leaned over me. "I love you so

much, Sean. It's been hell being apart from you."

"I know," he said from above me. "I know exactly what you mean." Sean kissed me gently and ran his hands through my hair; touching me like I was a goddess. I realized that he was making love to me in a different way than before. It was obvious that he was madly in love with me. He felt the same way that I did, and my heart began to throb at the realization.

He broke our kiss and pressed his forehead against mine while holding himself above my body with my legs around his waist. I felt him move inside me slowly, and I moaned as he stretched my insides. I grabbed his arms as he moved further inside and I whispered his name.

"You feel amazing, Scar," he whispered when we was entirely within me.

"Sean." I gasped as he moved inside of me. It felt amazing and right, completely different than the last time. I knew I could do that for the rest of my life. "Oh god," I whispered to him.

"I know," he said as he moved inside of me.

I grabbed his back and ran my hands down his flank then back through his hair. "You feel perfect," I said.

"Only for you," he whispered. Sean quickened his pace slightly and his lips were on mine again. He made love to me until I felt my body give into the all-consuming pleasure and I climaxed, whispering his name as he moved deeper into me.

"Sean, don't stop," I whispered through my tears. No one had ever made love to me like that before. I was so happy that

Sean was the first. Sean understood my tears were from happiness, not sadness or pain, and he kissed them away while still moving inside of me.

"I'll never stop," he said as he reached his own euphoria and released inside of me. "For the rest of my life, Scar."

Sean didn't move away or pull out. He stayed on top of me and kissed me tenderly, showing his love for me in his embrace alone. I ran my hands through his hair while I stared into his eyes, understanding that he was mine forever. Sean finally pulled away and lay down beside me. I moved closer and wrapped my body around his. He kissed me on the head.

"Why didn't we do that before?" I asked.

"I have no idea." He smiled. "We shouldn't have waited so long." Sean grabbed my hand and held it within his own. "You are everything to me, Scarlet. I'm just a walking shadow without you."

"I am too."

"I wish I didn't have to leave tomorrow."

I sighed. "I know."

"It's going to be a shitty five days."

"We can still talk every day," I said.

"It's not the same as seeing you every day," he said. I immediately thought of Ryan and knew our relationship would change if I did leave—it couldn't stay the same. But now I couldn't live without Sean. "You need to make a decision soon, Scar. I don't think I can put up with this for a long time. I may just drag you back to New York."

"I'll figure it out, babe." I hugged him tighter.

"We should go back in the living room," he said.

"I want to do it again," I said quickly.

Sean smiled at me. "I'm not a machine," he said. "I need a break before we go another round."

"But we'll do it again?" I asked earnestly.

"We can do it for the rest of our lives."

I smiled at him. "Let's lay in here for a while."

He laughed. "Okay, Scar. I'll make love to you again as soon as I'm ready."

"I don't want to make love."

His eyes shined a brighter shade. "Then what do you want to do?"

"I want you to fuck me."

Sean's breathing increased. "I love making love to you."

"I know," I said. "But I also know you enjoy fucking me. And I enjoy it, too." I trailed my hand up his chest then tickled the skin.

"I can't say that I'm displeased by the idea."

I smiled. "I know you aren't." I grabbed his fully erect penis and massaged it. "I want it, Sean. And just because it's carnal doesn't mean there is less love in it. I know you love me."

He swallowed the lump in his throat. "I love you more than anything."

"And I feel the same way."

He cupped my face and looked at my lips. Then, he leaned

in and kissed me gently, massaging my mouth with this own. His hand slid up my thigh until his thumb rested on my clit. He rubbed me the same way he did last time. I immediately began to shake for him.

"You like this?"

"Yeah."

He leaned down and licked me in the same area his fingers were. "You really like it."

I nodded as I bit my lip.

"Sit up."

I did as he commanded and he moved behind me. He grabbed my breasts and pinched the nipples while he separated my legs with his. I was sitting on his lap and I felt his dick against my back. I was shaking with excitement. He kissed my neck then trailed his lips to my ear.

"I know I'm a little bigger than normal," he whispered. "And you are very tight."

I moaned at his words.

"And this is going to make it feel even fuller. But you are so wet, I don't think it will matter."

I reached behind me and ran my fingers through his hair. I felt his breaths fall on my shoulder as he kissed my neck. The tip of his penis was leaking fluid and it stuck to my back. I didn't mind. It was hot.

He grabbed my hips and lifted me slightly. Then, he pulled me down slowly onto his dick. I felt myself expand as I took him in. Sean encouraged me to move, but he left me to determine how quickly I wanted him inside me.

"Oh god, Sean," I said as I moved down. "Sean."

"Yeah," he whispered.

I moaned louder as he pressed his entire length inside of me.

"You are almost there, Scar."

"You're huge, Sean."

He chuckled. "Thank you."

I finally felt him stop moving as he was completely sheathed. "God."

He began to thrust inside of me very slowly. "How does this feel?"

"Oh, Sean. Yes, yes."

He grabbed my hips and started to thrust harder. I watched his reflection in the mirror on the closet. He stared at my ass while he fucked me. His chest started to drip with sweat and the sight was enough to make me come.

I grabbed his thigh as he pounded into me. "I'm about to come."

He looked in the mirror and stared at my reflection. "Come for me. I want to watch you."

"Fuck me harder."

He did. He thrust into me with a greater speed. "Come on, Scar."

I screamed his name as the tidal wave of pleasure hit me.

He continued to pound into me as I rode the high. "Sean. Sean. Fuck yeah."

"Fuck yes," he said as he watched me. "Fuck, Scar. I love watching you come." He grabbed my hips and started to tense as he had his orgasm. He locked his gaze to mine as he started to come. "Scarlet. Scarlet. Yes, Scarlet." He finished with his final thrusts. "Yes."

When he was done, we stayed that way for a moment, both breathing heavily. He kissed my neck then my cheek. His hands caressed me everywhere, confessing his love for me silently. "I love fucking you, Scar."

"I love it, too."

"Did I hurt you?"

I laughed. "God, no. I loved it."

He smiled. "I'm glad. I know you aren't used to my size yet."

"Is that a challenge?"

His eyes twinkled. "Are you asking me to break you in?"

I nodded. "Please."

"I would love to. You will be perfectly molded to my cock."

"Good," I said. "Because my body is only for you."

"And mine's only for you."

4

The front door opened and closed around eleven that night, and Ryan walked into the living room.

"Hey," he said as he sat down on the couch next to us. Sean and I were making out while we watched a movie, but we broke apart when we heard the door open.

"How was the show?" I asked.

"It was good," he said. "Cortland and I laughed a lot."

I nodded. "You didn't meet any girls?"

He shook his head. "None that I wanted," he said. "By the way, I'm having a girl over. She'll be gone before you wake up in the morning, so you don't have to worry about seeing her."

"Is she as lovely as that last girl?" I asked.

Ryan smiled. "She has a lot of tattoos, if that's what you are asking."

"So you just call them and they come over?"

"Yes," he said. "They are open to casual sex."

I shook my head. "Ryan, you need to find someone serious. Stop messing around with these inked girls."

"I already said I can't find anyone," he said. "Introduce me to someone. I'm willing to do a blind date."

"I don't have any friends," I said. "At least not in Seattle."

"Hang in there," Sean said. "You'll find someone."

"I hope so," Ryan said. "I'm tired of being pestered by my little sister, who didn't get a real boyfriend until yesterday."

"I hope you find what I've found, Ryan."

My brother looked at me and Sean. "Me too," he said quietly. He walked down the hallway and disappeared. Sean started kissing me again and we made out on the couch until there was a knock on the door. Ryan answered it and a girl came into the apartment. As soon as the door was opened, Ryan and she were going at it against the wall. Ryan pulled away and they walked to his bedroom.

I shook my head and started kissing Sean again. "Let's go in my room."

"No," Sean said quickly. "Your brother is in the next room."

We both heard the headboard slam into the wall and the girl start moaning in Ryan's room. I stared at Sean. "I don't think he cares." I laughed.

"It's still disrespectful."

The headboard crashing into the wall echoed throughout the house. "He won't even notice," I said.

Sean laughed. "He has a lot of built up sexual energy, doesn't he?"

"Well, he's been babysitting me for the past few weeks," I said as I got up. My shirt fell from my body and I pulled down my pants, standing in just my underwear and bra in front of him. Then, I carried my clothes into my bedroom. After I got into bed, Sean came into the room and closed the door behind him. I smiled in victory as he took off his clothes and crawled on top of me. Ryan and his friend could be heard through the walls, and it made us both laugh.

"He knows we can hear him, right?" Sean asked.

"He isn't stupid," I said as I pulled his lips to mine.

"Well, most of the time you act like he is."

"That's because he is."

Sean pulled away. "Is this weird?" he asked hesitantly.

"It is," I said. "You are lying on top of a girl, who is naked and damn fine, and all you care about is my brother?"

Sean smiled at me then leaned over. Our lips were glued together again as Sean inserted himself within me and moved delicately, making love to me like last time. After a few moments, it became more carnal. Because we were making out on the couch for the entire movie, we were both ready for more. Sean pounded into me harder than last time, which I didn't mind in the least. I rocked my hips from below, beckoning him to thrust into me faster. Not only were we making love, but we were releasing our sexual desire for one another. I trusted him and didn't mind being so overtly sexual with him. "I want it harder, Sean." I moaned.

He picked up his pace. "You got it, babe."

I scratched his back as he brought me to climax. "Sean." I breathed. "I love you."

Sean released himself into me with his final thrusts while saying my name. He grabbed my hips and lifted them from the bed, pushing himself inside of me as far as possible. It was the hottest thing I had ever seen. "Scarlet," he whispered while he filled me. "My Scarlet." Sean stayed on top of me as he caught his breath.

"You are amazing under the sheets," I said.

"It takes two to tango," he whispered. "I love making love to you."

I licked the sweat away from his chest. "That makes two of us."

Sean lay beside me for a moment. "I should go back in the living room before Ryan—finishes."

I laughed. They could still be heard through the wall. It sounded like the building was being demolished. "Sleep with me," I said. "I miss sleeping with you."

"I do too," he said. "But I have to stay out there. I don't want Ryan to know I've been in your room with you—making love to his sister."

"It's none of his business."

"It's his apartment."

"That I pay for," I retorted.

Sean kissed my head. "I know how important he is to you. I don't want to mess this up."

"I know." I sighed. "But I'm sleeping with you tonight— even if that means I have to sleep on the couch."

"You don't have to do that."

"I want to," I said as I kissed him.

We dressed ourselves and went back into the living room. The blankets and pillows were on the couch and we curled up in each other's arms. The noise from Ryan's room abated for a while, but then the racket returned with full force.

"I don't think we are going to get any sleep tonight." I sighed.

"That's okay," he said. "As long as I'm with you, I don't care."

Sean held me to his chest while we snuggled in the dark. We would kiss for a few minutes, but then we would break apart and start talking. Then, we would go back to kissing again. Finally, around three in the morning, the noise from Ryan's bedroom stopped and we were able to fall asleep. Sean and I didn't mind the loud distraction because we had a great time talking and cuddling, enjoying our moments together before Sean had to leave the next morning. Eventually, we fell asleep in each other's arms until Sean's alarm went off the next morning and we were awoken from our slumber.

Sean rose from the couch and turned off the alarm on his phone. Ryan was already sitting at the kitchen table, reading the newspaper. I wondered why he was awake so early. The guy never slept in for any reason. Sean started packing his stuff into his bag then headed to the shower. I changed into my street clothes and ate cereal at the table while I waited for Sean.

Ryan put down the paper and looked at me. "Is he leaving today?"

I nodded, too depressed to respond verbally.

"Why aren't you going with him?" he asked.

"I don't know," I said. "I'm not ready yet."

He stared at me for a moment. "You seem happy with him, Scarlet—really happy. I think you should move back to New York."

"You do?" I asked.

Ryan nodded. "Please don't stay here because of me," he said. "I have a feeling that's what's holding you back."

I sighed. "I'm not just staying because of you, Ryan—I want to stay. I'm afraid if I move back to New York, we'll lose touch again—and—I just can't do that to you again. I love being here with you—even when you make fun of me."

Ryan smiled. "I love having you here, Scarlet. Having you here has been amazing, and I wish you didn't have to go, but I know you love him and you should be with him. What kind of brother would I be if I let you stay with me just so I could be happy?"

"You are the best brother anyone could ask for, Ryan."

"I know," he whispered. "And you are the best sister."

"But everything will be different," I said. "I will only see you a few times a year, if that."

"That's what happens when you grow up," he said sadly.

"Come to New York. You can live with me and Sean. He won't mind."

"My shop is here, Scar."

"Start a new one."

"It doesn't work like that."

"I'll support you."

"Now you are just castrating me." He laughed. He reached across the table and grabbed my hand. "It's okay, Scarlet—really. I want you to go."

Sean came back into the living room and Ryan released my hand. My brother stared at me, waiting for me to tell Sean that I was moving back to New York, but I couldn't say it. I was torn. I didn't want to leave my brother, but I wanted to be with Sean.

"Are you ready?" Sean asked me.

"Yes," I said as I rose from the chair. Ryan got to his feet and stared at me for a moment longer then dropped his gaze and turned to Sean.

"Have a safe flight," he said as he shook Sean's hand.

Sean nodded. "Thanks for letting me stay here."

"You are family, Sean—you are always welcome." Ryan sat down at the table and Sean and I left through the front door. We took a cab to the airport and I walked with Sean as far as security would let me. The gate to his plane was across the room and the passengers were boarding, but Sean stayed with me until the last minute.

My tears fell even though I tried my best to fight them. Sean hugged me for a long moment before he walked away.

"I love you," he whispered. "It's only for a few days."

"I'm sorry," I said as I wiped away my tears. "I can't help

it. I'm going to miss you."

He kissed my lips. "I'll miss you too, babe."

"I love you so much," I whispered.

"I know," he said. "We'll talk every day. It's going to be okay."

The last call sounded over the intercom, and Sean kissed me one last time. "I have to go."

"I know," I said. "I love you."

"I love you, Scar." He dropped my hand and walked away. I watched him until he vanished inside the gate then I turned around and went back home, wiping my tears away until the cab stopped in front of the apartment. I waited in the lobby until I found my bearings then I went up and into the living room.

Ryan stared at me for a moment with pity in his eyes. I knew he wanted to say something, but he held it back, saving it for a time when I wasn't so emotional. I disappeared into my room and didn't come out for the rest of the day.

5

The next morning, I went to the tattoo parlor with Ryan and got his appointments ready for the day. While he was with the customers, I went down to the bank and dropped off the money that Ryan had made the day before. If he was robbed again, the criminals wouldn't have much to take. The money wasn't a lot, but it was enough to cover his rent on the property and the extra bills he had at the place. Business wasn't as good as it was before the last break in, despite the website that we made, but I knew it would pick up eventually.

The money I was making from editing was covering the rent, utilities, our phone bills, and our food, but I still didn't have enough money to make a single payment towards my loan. Ryan nagged me about it, saying we could borrow money from someone else to make a payment, but I rejected the idea. I would rather steal money from the government than a friend.

"I need to go to work," I said as I cleaned up the counters and locked the safe in the back.

"Do you mean that you are going home?" he asked while he cleaned his equipment.

"No," I said. "My office is at Mega-Shake."

Ryan laughed. "You are going to get fat," he said. "Good thing you play ball with me and Cortland."

"Well, I'll see you later," I said as I walked out of the shop. I took a cab across town and sat in my usual booth by the window. A manuscript had come in the day before and I started to work on it, needing to get paid as soon as possible. My editing service was becoming reputed as a prestigious company, thanks to Christine Dirkson, and I was getting more clients because of it. Now that I was getting quicker at reading the manuscripts, I planned to make a payment on my loans soon. Hopefully, they would allow an extension until then. Ryan wasn't making any money and I was our sole supporter. That was another reason why I couldn't leave him. What would he do?

My phone rang and I grabbed it immediately, hoping Sean was calling me, but my face fell when I saw Cortland's name. I took the call.

"Hey," I said sadly.

"You sound depressed."

"I thought you were Sean."

Cortland laughed. "Thanks," he said. "What are you doing?"

"I'm working at Mega-Shake."

"I'm right down the street," he said. "I'll just swing by."

"Okay," I said before I hung up.

Cortland walked in the door a few moments later wearing his gym clothes. "Hey," he said. "I was down at the courts with some friends."

I sniffed the air. "I can tell."

"Your brother was right—you are a brat."

I smiled at him. "How are you?"

"Good," he said. "I'm taking Monnique out later."

"Are you official yet?"

"No." He sighed. "I don't want to scare her off by acting too needy. I'm waiting until she gives me some indication that she wants to be in a relationship. I really don't want to mess this up."

"So you haven't slept with her either?"

"No," he said. "Like I said, I don't want to fuck it up, even though I would love to sleep with her. She seems like she would be a heathen in bed."

I stared at him for a moment, uncomfortable by his obvious sexual energy.

"Sorry." He smiled. "I haven't gotten laid since I was with you."

"That's understandable," I said.

"Are you doing okay?" he asked.

"Yeah." I sighed. "I miss him, but it isn't so bad."

"Are you moving there or what?"

I closed my computer. Obviously, I wasn't going to get any work done. "I don't know, Cortland. I don't know."

Cortland stared at me for a moment. He reached out and ran his fingers over the top of my hand. "I didn't mean to upset you," he said gently.

"It's not you, Cortland. I'm sorry that I snapped. I just don't know what to do. The idea of leaving you and Ryan makes me want to cry. I can't stand not seeing you guys every day."

"Don't you feel that way about Sean?" he asked.

"Of course I do," I said. "I miss him so much."

"I hate to be blunt about it, but you have to choose one. You can't have both, Scarlet."

"I can't leave Ryan," I said. "It hurt him so much last time, and I can't do that again. We are close—closer than we have ever been, and I don't want to ruin that. He is the only family I have left."

Cortland sighed. "Ryan will understand if you want to leave. I know him, Scar. He would rather see you happy than let you be miserable."

"I'm not miserable," I whispered. "I just want to go as much as I want to stay."

"That's some hard luck."

"And Ryan needs me," I said. "I can't just abandon him right now. His shop is barely breaking even. He hasn't even paid off the old equipment that was stolen."

"He can live with me," Cortland said. "You wouldn't be abandoning him."

"He would never accept that, Cortland. You know that. He only accepts my help because we are family."

"I don't know what to say," Cortland said. "Maybe you could stay until his shop starts to make money again. That gives him enough time to accept the fact that you are leaving, and it also gives him some cushion financially. That sounds fair."

"But even then I don't want to go."

Cortland sighed. "I don't know what to tell you, Scar. The only way you get what you want is if Sean moves here, but you already said he wouldn't."

"I can't ask him to do that," I said. "It would be hard for him to find work here, and he's been at his firm for years. Besides, he loves Manhattan."

"I have a feeling he loves you more."

I shook my head. "I can't ask him to do that."

Cortland sighed. "Then you lose Sean as your boyfriend— permanently—or you don't see Ryan like you used to. I think the choice is clear, Scar. Learn from your mistakes. Make an effort to stay in contact with Ryan and you won't mess it up again."

I leaned back in my chair and crossed my arms over my chest. "I'm done discussing this."

Cortland nodded. "Can I buy you a milkshake?" he asked.

"I'm trying to cut back." I smiled. "Even though I play basketball with you guys, I'm starting to gain weight."

Cortland nodded. "We do eat here a lot," he said as he looked around the place. He turned his gaze back to me. "Did Sean ever ask if you slept with anyone?"

"No," I said. "I hope he doesn't."

Cortland nodded. "I like Sean," he said. "I don't want him to have a beef with me."

"Neither do I," I said. "It would be very childish of him. But then again, if I knew he hung out with a woman he slept with, it would make me uncomfortable. I trust him, but I would rather not know about it."

"I suppose," he said. "You seem really happy when you're with him."

I smiled. "Yes, I am."

"I am happy for you," he said. "Did he still refuse to sleep with you?"

I shook my head. "I can't believe Ryan told you that."

Cortland smiled. "The guy tells me everything. So, what's the story? Are you too much for him?"

I laughed. "He said he wanted to take it slow, make sure that I trusted him before we started a physical relationship."

"And he kept it up?"

"No." I laughed. "I broke him down. He wouldn't give it up, but I eventually won."

Cortland laughed. "That sounds about right," he said. "I've been there, done that. So how was it?"

"It was amazing," I said. "It was the best sex I've ever had."

"That's because you are in love with him and he feels the same way."

"Well, it makes a huge difference."

"I hope Monnique and I are that way when we get together. I can see myself falling in love with her. I just don't want to get emotionally attached to her if she doesn't feel the same way."

"She will, Cortland. You are an amazing guy."

"Thanks," he said. "And since we've slept together—twice—I'll take your word for it. It just doesn't mean the same thing coming from my mom."

I laughed. "I can see why." My phone started ringing and I smiled when I saw that it was Sean. I answered the phone with a smile in my voice. "Hey, babe."

"Hey," he said. "I wanted to talk to you before I turned in for the night."

"How was your day?"

"Uneventful, boring, blah," he said with a laugh. "I went to the gym after work, which I haven't done in a long time, then I cooked myself dinner. Now I'm getting ready to do it again tomorrow. How was your day?"

"Pretty much the same," I said. "I helped Ryan at the shop for a few hours."

"What are you doing now?"

"Working at Mega-Shake."

Sean sighed. "I'm not trying to be annoying, but I don't like you walking home alone after dark," he said.

"Cortland is here," I said. "He'll walk me home."

"Good," he said. "Just don't make it a habit."

"I won't," I said. "I miss you."

"I miss you, too."

"We'll be together again soon," I whispered.

"That moment can't come soon enough," he said.

"I'll let you go," I said. "I know that you're tired."

"Okay." He sighed. "I love you, Scar."

"I love you, too."

I hung up the phone and felt my heart fall. Ending the call was the hardest part. Cortland caught my saddened expression. "It looks like you've made your choice."

I smiled at him. "It seems like I have."

Cortland leaned back in his seat. "Are you ready to go home?" he asked. "It sounded like Sean wants me to take you."

"If you don't mind," I said.

"I never mind," he said.

We left the restaurant and drove up the street. Cortland pulled over and we both got out of the car.

"You don't need to walk me to the door," I said.

"I have a feeling that Sean would disagree with that," he said. "I really don't mind, Scar. Besides, I can say hi to Ryan."

We walked to the apartment and I unlocked the door. Ryan was in the shower when we went into the living room, so Cortland decided to hang around.

"Are you going to tell him?"

"What?" I asked.

"About your plan?" he said. "That you'll stick around until the shop is prosperous, but then you'll be leaving? I think giving him enough time to deal with it will make it easier for him to let you go. That's just my suggestion. But either way, he'll be happy for you, Scar. I know he will."

"Thanks," I said.

Ryan came into the room and smiled when he saw Cortland. "Hey," he said. "What are you doing here?"

"I just brought Scarlet home and thought I would stick around for a while."

"How's it going with Monnique?" he asked.

"Good," Cortland said. "I'm taking her out tonight."

"Has she put out yet?" Ryan asked.

"Ryan!" I said.

Cortland laughed. "No, she hasn't."

"Just make sure you look good tonight," he said. "Wearing the right clothes will make any girl open her legs."

"Can you not see me?" I asked my brother.

"Since I actually like this girl, I was hoping that she would want to commit first," Cortland said. "I want to settle down, especially with her."

Ryan nodded. "She sounds like the real thing."

"You have no idea." Cortland smiled.

I turned to Ryan. "I can't believe you told Cortland what Sean said the other day."

"I figured you were going to tell him anyway," he said. "He's your best friend, right?"

"Well, Sean is now," I said. "But you still shouldn't have told him that."

"It's too late now." Ryan sat on the couch next to Cortland.

I turned to Cortland. "Ryan has sex really, really loud. He practically demolished the apartment the other night."

Cortland shrugged then gave Ryan a high-five. "That's awesome."

I rolled my eyes at them. "You guys are annoying."

"Well, you slept with Cortland, so I know he can't be that irritating," Ryan jabbed.

"I thought we weren't discussing that again?" I said. "And please don't tell Sean. I don't want him to act weird around Cortland."

"You know I would never do that," my brother said.

"Well, you just told Cortland that Sean wouldn't sleep with me."

"What?" He laughed. "I thought it was funny."

I stared at him. "I thought you respected him for it."

"I do," he said. "But I also thought it was funny."

Ryan and Cortland started watching a game that was on and we said nothing for a while. When a commercial came on, Cortland met my gaze, silently encouraging me to tell Ryan that I was leaving, but I couldn't do it. It was such a delicate situation. Even though Ryan would never admit it, he would be miserable after I left.

Eventually Cortland gave up and rose from his chair. "I need to get ready for my date," he said as he walked to the front door.

"Have a good night," I said.

"I hope you score," Ryan added.

"Thanks," Cortland said before he shut the door.

Ryan and I sat on the couch and said nothing for a long time. Finally, Ryan turned to me. "I really appreciate everything you have done for me, Scar, and not just the money thing, but everything. I don't want you to leave, but I think you should go. I'll be fine, Scar."

"I don't want to," I whispered.

"You have to, Scarlet."

"No."

"Sean is your everything now. I can't always be the man in your life."

I sighed. "I know."

"I'll support whatever decision you make," he said. "But please do what makes you happy. If you aren't happy, then I'm not happy."

I nodded.

"And I think you should tell Sean your decision when he gets here in a few days," he said. "Let him know what's going on. I see how miserable you are without him. I sincerely hope that you choose him and fly back to New York with him when he leaves."

"I'll think about it."

He stared at me for a moment then dropped his gaze. "Okay."

6

Sean

Even though Scarlet and I weren't together, she was still the first thing on my mind when we were apart. My decision to commit to her was the best one I had ever made. I should have done it sooner. Everything was so easy and natural with her. We had a great time together without even trying, and I loved being a part of her family. Cortland was a cool guy, too.

When I was at work, I told Brian everything that happened. He was happy for me, but I could also tell he was bummed out. He had been crushing on Scarlet forever and now she was officially off limits. She was mine.

"What about Penelope?" he asked when he got into the elevator after work.

"What about her?" My voice came out harsher than I meant it to.

"You broke up only a few weeks ago," he said. "Are you sure you should be in another relationship?"

"I don't know," I said honestly. "But I love Scarlet. I want to be with her."

"Does she know that you aren't over Penelope?"

"I guess," I said. "I didn't actually say it, but I'm sure she inferred it. Besides, I'll get over her soon. I'm happy with Scarlet."

Brian sighed. "I don't know."

"You're just mad because you wanted Scarlet first."

He smiled. "That may have something to do with it," he said. "But you're right. Scarlet is way better than Penelope. It seems like that girl never loved you. She has already been dating a guy I know on Wall Street. In fact, she was probably with him before you even broke up."

I tried to control the emotions charging through my body. I still loved Penelope and missed her. His news was a stab to the heart. Obviously, she was already fucking someone new, had been for a long time, but I didn't want to hear about it. "I wouldn't doubt it," I forced myself to say.

"But Scarlet is cool," Brian said. "She is funny and sexy at the same time. How is she in bed?" he asked. "You have to tell me."

I glared at him and he stepped away. "Talk about my girlfriend like that again and I'll beat the shit out of you."

Brian smiled. "I didn't mean to offend you," he said. "I was just wondering."

"Well, stop wondering."

"Okay," he said. "Since you aren't with Penelope anymore and she cheated on you, tell me about her. What was she like in the sack?"

I glared at him again. "Don't talk about *any* of my girlfriends that way."

Brian rolled his eyes. "You're no fun anymore."

The elevator doors opened and we walked out to the sidewalk. "I'll see you tomorrow," I said as I walked in the opposite direction as Brian, trying to get away from him. I called down a cab and headed towards my apartment. Knowing that Penelope was with some other guy made me want to die. I hated the way I felt about her. I still loved her.

When I got into the apartment, I picked up the ring on the kitchen table and opened the box, staring at the diamonds. After a moment, I closed it and tossed it back on the table. It was evident that Penelope was never coming back to me. She was gone. It was time to get rid of the ring, but I still didn't reach for it. I sighed and took a shower instead. When I got out, I called Scarlet and melted at the sound of her voice. I missed her so much. This long-distance relationship was already killing me. I wanted to be with her always, and not just because she quieted my pain, but because I loved being with her. I sat in the living room, looking for something to watch on the television, when a knock on the door made me jump. It was late at night and I wasn't sure who would come to my apartment at that hour. When I saw the person on the other side of the door through the peephole, I almost didn't answer it. It was Penelope.

Against my better judgment, I unlocked the bolt and opened the door.

Her brown locks curved around her face and complemented her features perfectly. The green eyes that I adored stared at me, and the light of the hallway glinted in her irises, making them appear to be on fire. My heart was beating so fast I thought I would fall over and die right then and there. There was no reason I could think of that she would come to me. I glanced to her ring finger and noticed that she wasn't wearing an engagement ring. I assumed that she wouldn't have left me for someone unless she was tying the knot. She didn't say anything and I remained silent, waiting for her to speak first. Honestly, I wouldn't have known what to say anyway.

"Hey," she said as she tucked a strand of hair behind her ear. After everything she did to me, I still thought she was beautiful and I hated it. Her flawless skin was enough of a distraction from my logical thought. The uncontrollable reaction she inflicted in me was making me furious. I hated being under this girl's spell.

"What do you want?" I asked bluntly. She flinched at the venom in my voice, but I didn't care. That bitch broke my heart and wasted my commitment. I could have been with Scarlet the whole time. The thought of Penelope and her new boyfriend rekindled the anger inside of me. "You must have me confused with your current boyfriend," I snapped. "I'm the guy you dumped. Remember?"

Penelope stared at me for a moment. "Can I talk to you, Sean?"

"What are we doing now?"

She sighed. "Can I come in?"

"No." I started to close the door, but she held it open.

"Please?" she asked.

The look in her eyes made me release my hold on the door. No matter what she did to me, I still couldn't just push her out of my apartment. I pushed the door open and let her walk in. The door slammed behind her.

"To what do I owe the pleasure?" I said sarcastically.

"I know you're mad, Sean, and you have every right to be. I'm not here to dissuade your anger."

"Then what the fuck do you want?" I snapped. "I'm with Scarlet now and I love her. You don't need to pity me, Penelope. I've moved on."

"You're dating Scarlet?" she asked sadly.

The sadness in her voice made me happy. I hoped she was jealous. "Yes," I said. "And I love her."

Penelope looked down. "Sean, I need to tell you something," she whispered. "I made a mistake when I left you and I regret it. I was hoping that we could talk things out."

"Is this a joke?" I snapped. "I don't want you, Penelope."

"Sean, listen to me."

"No," I said. "I'm done with you. Get out of my apartment and my life."

"Sean," she said as she grabbed my arms. I didn't pull away and I hated myself for it. "I'm pregnant."

My body remained immobile at her words. Of all the things I thought she was going to say, that was what I least expected. "You are *pregnant*?"

She nodded. "And it's yours, Sean."

I shook my head, battling the confusion raging in my mind. "How can I be sure of that?"

Penelope sighed. "When I went to the doctor, he said I was four weeks along," she said. "You are the only person I slept with at that time. When my boyfriend found out it wasn't his, he didn't want to be with me anymore."

I started pacing the apartment, processing everything she just said. Penelope was pregnant with my kid. I was going to be a fucking dad. My body continued to pace around the living room as my mind went somewhere else. Penelope watched me move, but didn't say anything.

"I'm sorry," she said. "I didn't know you were dating Scarlet."

I didn't respond to her words as I continued to walk.

"Please say something," she said.

"What am I supposed to say?"

"Do you want to be involved?" she asked. "I understand if you don't. And if you do want to be involved, but not be in a relationship, that's fine as well. But I've realized how wrong I was and that I made a mistake. We were getting really serious and I got cold feet, running to the first guy that would have me. I love you, Sean, and I'm so sorry about what I did to you. Please take me back."

"I can't," I said. "I have Scarlet."

Penelope sighed. "I know and I feel terrible about that," she said. "But you and I are going to have a baby, Sean. Shouldn't we try to be a family?"

I stared at her for a moment while thoughts flashed across my mind. Marrying Penelope was exactly what I wanted; having her carry my child was even better. This wasn't the way I wanted it to play out, but perhaps that's where I was meant to be. Maybe it was a sign. Penelope was carrying my child and wanted to work on our relationship. She said she was sorry for everything. But then I thought of Scarlet and everything I had with her. She was everything to me. I couldn't live without her. I still loved Penelope, but I loved Scarlet more. I never wanted to be the dad that was separated from the mother, but I couldn't do that to Scarlet. I couldn't leave her.

"I can't trust you, Penelope."

She grabbed my hand. "I know," she said. "But I'll spend my life making it up to you." Her eyes started to saturate with tears and drip down her face. "I wish I could take it back, but I can't, Sean, and I'm sorry. I regret everything. Please give me another chance. I promise you won't regret it." The tears streamed down her face and I watched them fall. Even after everything that she did to me, I still hated seeing her in pain. "I love you, Sean. I've always loved you."

As I listened to her words, I imagined the life I always wanted. It wasn't perfect and the way we came to this situation was painful, but we were still there. I still cared for Penelope, but I wanted Scarlet. But then my future son or daughter was in my life.

Could I really do that to them? Be married to another woman and have other kids? I would never want my child to experience that. It would make me a horrible person. Shouldn't I try to make this work for my kid? I hated everything about the situation. I wanted to die because of what I was about to do to Scarlet. I wanted to fucking die. I met her gaze and watched her for a moment. "I love you too," I whispered.

She kissed my hand and held it in her own. "Thank you," she said. Penelope wrapped her arms around me and I held her. My heart ached for the woman that I loved. Seeing her shed those tears for me was a declaration of her love and remorse. If Penelope wasn't carrying my child, I would have turned her away, but since she was, I wanted to give the relationship another chance. Of course I wanted to be in the child's life—that was obvious, but I would rather do that as Penelope's husband than her boyfriend. It isn't exactly what I wanted, but I was stuck. I was going to be a dad.

My thoughts of Scarlet pained me. I knew how much this would hurt her, but a part of me knew she would understand, knowing that the pregnancy changed everything. I loved Scarlet, I really did, and I felt my heart ache because I wouldn't be spending my life with her. She was everything to me, and now I would lose her forever. She wouldn't want to be friends with me—maybe never speak to me again—but she would understand.

Penelope pulled away and spotted the engagement box sitting on the kitchen table. She was still for a moment then she grabbed it. Her eyes lit up when she saw the ring inside. She must have spotted the engraving because she knew it was hers. "It's beautiful, Sean." Tears sprung from her eyes. She put the ring on her finger. I didn't even ask her. But the sight made me happy. She was serious about raising this kid with me—as a family. I wanted the best for my child—nothing less. He would have family vacations, ball games in the park, and a father to look up to, someone who sacrificed the love of his life just to be perfect for him.

Penelope reached up to kiss me, but I pulled away. "I'm still with Scarlet," I said. "I'm committing to you for the rest of my life, but I'm with Scarlet until I end it. Nothing can happen until I talk to her."

Penelope nodded. "I understand," she said as she hugged me. "I love you, Sean, and I'm so sorry."

I returned her embrace. "I love you too," I said. "And I'm very excited about the baby."

"You are?" she asked as she pulled away, a look of surprise on her beautiful face.

"Of course," I said. "Why wouldn't I be?" I placed my hand over her slightly distended stomach. "I got a fiancé and a baby today."

Penelope smiled then tears fell from her eyes as she looked at me. I understood why she was so emotional. I just took her back to be a father to her child. I sacrificed my relationship with Scarlet, even though I didn't want to, just to commit to our unborn baby.

The baby was mine. It was my responsibility. I was forgiving her for everything and we were moving forward as a family. "I don't deserve you, Sean," she whispered.

I kissed her head, but said nothing. I knew she didn't deserve me, but that didn't matter anymore. The only thing that mattered was our child.

7

Scarlet

"When is Sean going to be here?" Ryan asked. He watched me check my hair in the mirror and make sure my makeup was perfect. "You look fine, Scar. It's just Sean."

"This is my boyfriend we are talking about—not just *Sean*," I said. "And he should be here any minute."

He rolled his eyes. "Do you want me out of the apartment for the evening?" he asked.

"No, of course not," I said quickly.

"I just assumed you would want to be alone."

"We do," I said. "But not all the time."

"Well, if you want me to visit Cortland, let me know."

"That won't be necessary." I laughed.

The knock on the door made me jump with excitement. "I got it!"

Ryan didn't move from the couch. "I couldn't care less," he said sarcastically.

I opened the door and jumped into Sean's arms, almost knocking him down from the force of my jump. He laughed as he staggered backwards. He dropped his bag on the ground and I started kissing him, pushing him against the wall as I grabbed his face and kissed him like it was the last time.

74

Sean moaned as he kissed me and I ran my hands over his body. When we finally broke our embrace, he was smiling at me. "Are you happy to see me?"

"Is it obvious?" I asked. "I was trying to play it cool."

"You never play it cool."

"No, I don't." I grabbed his face and kissed him again and we made out in the hallway for a few minutes. Sean pulled away from me and rested his head against mine. He was having a moment and I let him take it. I knew how much he missed me over the past five days.

"Is Ryan here?" he asked.

"Yes, unfortunately." I sighed. "But we are doing it anyway."

Sean smiled with his lips, but not his eyes. "I love you so much," he whispered. I saw the tears behind his eyes and I hugged him tightly. He wasn't this emotional when he left Seattle, but now he seemed to be overcome. Sean held me to his chest tightly and didn't let go for a long time.

I pulled away. "Let's get your stuff inside." I grabbed the one bag he had and it was practically empty. He didn't pack much. Sean grabbed the bag and placed it over his shoulder, following me inside. Sean moved to the living room and shook hands with Ryan. They started whispering about something but I couldn't make it out.

"So, what are you guys doing tonight?" Ryan asked.

"I don't know," I said as I wrapped my arms around Sean's

neck. "But I don't really care."

Sean rubbed his nose against mine and I immediately wanted to go in the bedroom. Ryan rose from the couch and grabbed his jacket from the coat rack. "I'll be at Cortland's," he said as he walked away. "Get this shit taken care of before I get back."

My lips were on Sean's and I was pulling him to the bedroom, wanting to be with him as soon as possible. Sean remained stationary as I tugged on his arm. The forlorn expression on Sean's face suddenly became apparent now that Ryan was gone. "What's wrong?"

Sean sighed as he took a seat on the couch. I sat beside him. Sean stared at me for a moment and I saw his eyes become coated with tears. Whatever had made Sean so upset was starting to frighten me. I didn't know what he was going to say.

He grabbed my face and kissed me gently. "I want you to know that I love you very much, Scarlet, and there is nothing I wouldn't do for you. You are everything to me—I mean it." He kissed me again and pulled away.

"You're scaring me," I whispered.

Sean grabbed my hand. "I have something to tell you."

My lungs took an involuntary breath, preparing for the battle about to be waged on my heart. Conversations that started with this phrase were always bad.

"Penelope came over last night and we started talking," he said quietly. I felt my heart race in my chest. I couldn't believe what was happening. "Penelope is pregnant with my baby, Scarlet."

I stared at him for a moment. "What?"

Sean nodded. "It's true."

"How do you know it's even yours?"

"Well, the sonogram said the conception was before the other guy. Plus, the guy left her when he found out it wasn't his. I think she's telling the truth."

I took a deep breath and sighed in relief. That wasn't what I was expecting Sean to say at all. I grabbed his hand and smiled at him. "I don't care, Sean. You should be in the baby's life if you want to be. This doesn't affect our relationship. I will love the baby like it was my own."

Sean closed his eyes and a tear fell down his cheek. He was completely moved by my words and I knew that he was frightened that I would end the relationship because of his child. I wanted to be with Sean—even if I was a stepmother.

"Scarlet." He breathed.

I grabbed his face and kissed his tears away then ran my hands through his hair, trying to calm him. "It's okay." I whispered.

Sean sighed before he continued. "I—I want to be in the child's life—of course I do. I wouldn't even consider anything else, but—but I want be a family, Scarlet. I—I can't do that to my kid, not at least try to be a family. I don't want to be two separate parents."

I stared at him. "You don't have to be with Penelope to raise this kid, Sean. Don't let her tell you otherwise. You can be a great father without being with her."

"But I don't want to do that to my child," he whispered. "I want to be a family."

My chest started rising and falling with my heightened fear. "What are you saying?" I asked.

Sean dropped his gaze. "I want to be a family, Scarlet. I don't want my kid to have a stepdad. I—I don't want that."

"Are you telling me that you want to be with Penelope?"

Sean was crying at this point. He wiped his tears away, but they continued to fall. "Yes."

I stood up and started pacing the room. "You came here to breakup with me," I whispered. "You'd already decided that you're going back to Penelope?"

Sean stood up and faced me. "I know you will understand, Scarlet. There is a child in this now. If she came to me without being pregnant, I would have thrown her out on her ass. I don't want her, Scar. I want you and no one else. But I have to try and make this work now. This is my responsibility. What kind of father would I be if I didn't try to make it work with Penelope? I don't want my kid to have to go back and forth between houses, spend the holidays at different places every year, or have step parents. If my parents divorced when I was little, it would have killed me, and I know kids often have emotional problems when their parents separate. I can't do that to my son or daughter. I know this ends our relationship, but now that I have a kid, that kid is my number one priority, even over you. Believe me, I don't want to lose you, and this arrangement is killing me. I don't want this, Scar. I really don't. I don't want Penelope. Please tell me you understand—I need to hear you say that."

I started to cry. "She is just going to fuck you over again, Sean. When she finds someone better that doesn't care that she already has a kid, she is going to leave you. Don't you get that? You are just going to end up divorced and alone. And I'm not going to be there when she breaks your heart again, Sean." I wiped my tears away and ran my hands through my hair. "I want nothing to do with you, Sean. You are picking her over me and you are making the wrong choice, Sean. The *wrong* choice."

"I'm not picking her over you!" he said. "I'm stuck with her. She is pregnant with *my* kid."

"I already heard you say that," I snapped. "And you can still be a great father without fucking the mom. Fuck you, Sean. You are going back to her because you want her. You've never gotten over her. This pregnancy just gives you an excuse."

"Please don't say that, Scar. You know that isn't true. You know how much I love you. I want to be with you. I mean it."

"Get the fuck out of my apartment and go back to where you came from," I said. "I never want to see you again—ever. I mean it. Don't call me or come back to Seattle. And don't you dare call my brother. After I tell him what you did, he is going to fucking kill you, Sean. We are done—for good. I hope you have a good life with your family. Now go." I turned around and let my tears fall without letting Sean see them. He didn't move for the door, but I waited for him to take his leave. I felt him stand behind me and touch my arm lightly.

"Please tell me that you understand," he whispered. "I need to hear you say that. I understand that you are angry—I am, too—but please tell me you understand."

"Don't touch me," I said as I jerked my arm away. "Now get the fuck out of my apartment."

He didn't move. I turned around and shoved him as hard as I could. Sean fell to the ground, but didn't retaliate. He rose to his feet and looked at me with tears dripping from his eyes.

"Have a good life, Sean. Go be with your *real* family."

Sean grabbed his bag and placed it over his shoulder. "I love you, Scar."

"Don't ever call me that again."

"I love you," he said. "I know you believe me." He turned around and left the apartment, closing the door gently behind him. When I heard the door shut, I collapsed on the ground and heaved with the heavy sobs that shook my body. My body convulsed with pain, and for the first time, I didn't want to go on—I didn't want to live. Sean made me so happy and now he betrayed me. Broke my heart into so many pieces, it looked like fairy dust. Hours went by as I laid in the living room, crying to myself. I remembered how depressed I was when I first got to Seattle and how much it hurt my brother. I didn't want to do that again. I'd made so much progress and I didn't want to falter again—I didn't want to fall.

My body lifted itself up and I stood in the middle of the apartment. The mirror on the wall showed my reflection of smeared makeup and running mascara. My hands wiped away the evidence of my tears, and I took a deep breath. I couldn't let myself fall again. Sean had betrayed me once, and it was my fault that I let him hurt me again. My life wouldn't spiral out of control like last time—I wouldn't let that happen.

My heart throbbed painfully for the trauma I'd just experienced, but I swallowed back the pain and decided that it wasn't worth it. Sean wasn't worth the pain even though we were perfect together and it felt so right. He was an idiot for throwing me away for a cheating bitch—even if she was carrying his baby. Sean and I were over. We were done. No amount of crying would change that. I walked into my bedroom and changed then I grabbed my jacket and left the apartment, heading for Cortland's place.

When I arrived there, Cortland answered the door with a smile on his face, but his expression fell when he realized how unhappy I was. "What's wrong?"

"Nothing," I said. "Can I come in?"

"Of course." He opened the door for me and allowed me to walk inside. Ryan was sitting on the couch with a dark-skinned woman. I recognized her immediately. She was gorgeous and exotic looking, and I completely understood Cortland's fascination with her.

"Where's Sean?" he asked.

I ignored him and walked into the living room. Ryan met my gaze and I knew he could read my expression clearly, unlike anyone else in the known world. He jumped from the couch and came to me, wrapping his arms around me tightly. Cortland watched us for a moment then turned to Monnique. "Something just came up," he said. "Can I take you home?"

I pulled away from Ryan. "No, that isn't necessary," I said quickly. I was moved that Cortland would risk offending his date just to comfort me, but I didn't want him to sacrifice anything for me. I turned to Monnique. "It's very nice to meet you. Cortland talks about you all the time."

She smiled at me. "I hope they are good things."

"Yes." I smiled. "Very good things."

Cortland turned to me. "Are you sure?"

"Yes," I said. "As long as I have Ryan, I'll be okay."

Ryan wrapped his arm around me and held me close to him. He kissed my forehead and let me bury my face in his shoulder. "I'm going to take her home," he said. "It was nice meeting you," he said to Monnique." We turned away and walked out of Cortland's apartment. Cortland followed us and he hugged me tightly before I left.

"Call me if you need anything—anything at all," Cortland said.

"I will." I smiled.

"I love you," he whispered.

"I love you, too."

Ryan wrapped his arm around my shoulder and we walked away, blending in with the darkness of the hallway. When we got to the street, I wasn't even watching where we were going, but since Ryan was with me, I didn't care. He guided me down the street until we reached Mega-Shake.

"I have a feeling we are going to need one," he said as he opened the door for me.

I took a seat and he ordered the milkshakes then brought them to the table.

Ryan stared at me and I could see the despair on his face. He hated seeing me in pain. "We don't have to talk about it," he said quietly. "But whenever you're ready, I'm here to listen."

"I love you," I said suddenly. "You have always been there for me when I don't deserve it—even now."

"That's because I love you more than anything," he said.

"Too bad Sean doesn't feel that way."

Ryan was trying to hide his anger, but some of it shined through. "That's because that fucker is an idiot."

I nodded. "Yes." The streets were deserted of people on that Friday night because of an approaching storm. The wind was practically blowing down the trees, but I was oblivious to it all. My thoughts were stuck on Sean.

"Did you get any new manuscripts?" he asked.

"Not today."

Ryan nodded.

"Penelope is pregnant with his baby so he left me for her,"

I blurted out. I knew Ryan wanted to know what happened and I didn't see the point in hiding it.

Ryan stared at me for a moment. "*What?*"

"He says he wants to try to be a family. I told him he could be in the child's life without being with Penelope, but he doesn't want that. He wants to make it work."

Ryan sat back and sighed. "I'm so sorry, Scar," he said. "I can't believe that. You seemed so happy together. I was really happy for you."

"I know," I whispered. "But he would rather be with her. She is just going to fuck him over like last time, but he is such an idiot that he doesn't get it. And when he falls, he'll be alone—I won't be there."

Ryan didn't say anything for a moment. He continued to look at me, waiting to see if I had anything more to say. "I think that what he did is wrong, Scarlet, but I also understand why he made that decision."

"Shut up, Ryan."

"I'm telling you what you need to hear," He snapped. "Some people are against raising children with separated parents— Sean might be one of those people."

"Fuck you."

He sighed. "I'm not saying what he did isn't wrong, Scar. *Listen to me.* But I understand why he did it. That's all I'm trying to say."

"No," I snapped. "He is just using this as an excuse so he

can go back to Penelope because he isn't over her. I don't think he gives a shit about that kid. It's probably not even his. It's always been Penelope—not me."

"Sean loves you, Scarlet. I know he does."

"You are being a really shitty brother right now."

Ryan closed his eyes and took a deep breath. It was obvious that he was getting frustrated with my catty remarks, but he didn't want to yell at me because of my obvious pain. "Do you think he would have left you if she wasn't pregnant?"

"Yes."

Ryan stared at me. "I don't think he would have."

"Well, I guess we'll never know."

Ryan sighed. "I'm pissed about what Sean did to you so don't think that I don't care. But I think it's best if I remain calm while you're emotional—it keeps you grounded."

"I hope Sean dies."

Ryan shook his head. "I know you don't mean that."

"Fuck yes, I do."

"Scarlet, this is an ugly color on you," he said. "Knock it off."

I stared at my brother then looked away. My brother was right. I was being childish. Sean just left me and I was entitled to be angry, but I was lashing out at everything—including my brother. "I'm sorry," I whispered.

"It's okay," he said. "Let's go home."

We threw our shakes away and walked back to the

apartment. When we were inside, I went into my bedroom and Ryan followed me. I got into the covers and he was about to lie on the floor beside me.

"Ryan, I'm fine," I said. "I don't need you to sleep in here."

"It's okay if you aren't fine, Scarlet."

"But I am," I said. "And I'm not just saying that."

"I don't mind sleeping with you."

"Well, I don't need you to."

Ryan stared at me for a moment and noticed the determination in my eyes. He got up and walked towards the door. "I'm down the hall if you change your mind."

"Good night."

"Good night, Scar," he said. "I love you."

"I love you, too."

Ryan left me alone in the darkness. I picked up my phone and turned it off, not wanting to talk to anybody. I probably wouldn't turn it on again—ever.

8

I was doing the bookkeeping at the shop while Ryan was working with his clients. I sighed when I realized that Ryan was still only breaking even. I didn't know when business would start picking up. The government hadn't contacted me again, and I hoped they forgot about me, which I knew was wishful thinking.

"How are the books?" Ryan asked as he walked behind the counter. My brother was being particularly nice to me since Sean dumped me. I appreciated his wing of protection, but I hated seeing him worry about me. I had already fallen low once, and I refused to do it again. My brother's fear of my depression just made me feel worse.

"They are the same." I sighed. "People just don't want tattoos right now."

Ryan sighed. "It'll pick up again," he said. "Business in unpredictable and constantly changing. Don't worry about it."

"Okay," I said.

Cortland walked in the door and nodded to Ryan. "You want to grab some grub?" he asked.

"No," Ryan answered. "I'm too busy right now. But take Scarlet."

"You're letting me leave for the day, boss?" I asked.

Ryan smiled at me. "Well, since you're working for free,

you can call all the shots."

"Or is it because I'm your sugar mama?" I said. "That's *why* I get to call all the shots."

Cortland laughed. "She has a point," he said. "Where do you want to go?"

"Whatever you want," I said. "I'm not very hungry."

Cortland thought for a moment. "How about a deli shop?" he asked.

"Sure," I said.

"We'll see you later," Cortland said to Ryan as we walked out. Cortland opened the door for me and we drove across town to a small sandwich shop. We ordered our food and Cortland paid before we sat down. I didn't even reach for my wallet. It was pointless.

Cortland looked at me. "You are finally learning." He smiled.

"That you're a douche?" I asked. "I picked up on that a long time ago."

Cortland laughed. "I'm glad that you are taking this breakup so well," he said. "It's only been a week and you are doing great. I know how much you loved him."

I wiped my mouth with a napkin. "It's his loss."

Cortland nodded. "You got that right," he said. "That bitch is a fucking idiot."

Cortland's words made me realize how mad he was about the whole thing. Ryan and Cortland tried to act calm and collected, but I knew they were furious about what happened. I was glad that they were acting normal. It was helping me get back to my center.

"Do you like your sandwich?" he asked.

I nodded. "It's good."

"Maybe you should drop it on the ground then eat it." He teased. "You might like it better that way."

I rolled my eyes. "I'm going to have to listen to this for the rest of my life, aren't I?"

"You just figured that out?"

I threw a chip at him and he caught it in his mouth. "Ta-da," he said with a slight bow.

I started laughing at the scene. My unstoppable laughter made Cortland laugh as well.

"You are so much fun to be around," he said as he ate his food.

"It takes two people to have a good time."

"And only one to start a party," he said. "How is the editing going?"

"Good," I said. "I made a payment towards my loan, but it's nowhere near the twenty percent mark."

"And how much is that?"

"Thirty grand," I said.

"Wow," he said. "Please let me lend you some money."

"No."

"Don't be stubborn."

"I have no idea if I will ever pay you back."

"And that's fine."

"No," I said. "Now drop it."

"Then what are you going to do?"

"Make as many payments as I can."

Cortland nodded. "My offer is always on the table."

"I know." I smiled. "And thank you."

Cortland stared at me for a moment. "Has he called?"

"No."

"That's probably for the best," he said. "I would hate to imagine Ryan intercepting that call."

"I would gladly hand it over." I smiled.

Cortland laughed. "Are you ready to go?" He pushed his food away.

"Yeah. I'm stuffed."

"I can tell, fatty."

"I'm a fine lady and I know it," I said.

"I love it when girls say that," he said as he opened the car door. "Most of the time, women just complain about their features." Cortland shut the door then got into the driver seat. "There's no point in complaining about something you can't change, so just shut up."

"Well, women are annoying."

Cortland drove back to the apartment and walked me to the door. "What are you going to do for the rest of the day?" he asked as we walked inside.

"I have another article to write for Mark and a manuscript

to finish, also known as rent money."

Cortland laughed. "I think it's awesome that you are helping Ryan so much," he said. "I know he really appreciates it."

"I know he does."

"The shop will be back to normal soon, and then you can take care of your loans," he said. "It's going to be okay."

I smiled at him. "I know it is."

Cortland left and I started working on the article for the Seattle Gazelle when the stab of melancholy hit. Fighting it grew more difficult as the days wore on. I missed Sean immensely, and the pain of his betrayal was too much to bear. Dreams of him woke me up in the middle of the night, and I cried myself back to sleep, wishing that we were still together. Cortland and Ryan were fooled. They really thought I was fine, but I was nothing of the sort. The truth is, I'd never felt worse.

9

Sean

Penelope moved in as soon as I got home. It was a drastic change, going from being with Scarlet to living with Penelope, my pregnant fiancé, but I knew it was necessary since we were getting married anyway. Penelope's stomach bulged out slightly, but I still thought she was beautiful and attractive.

The first time we made love, it was awkward. I thought about Scarlet. I forced the thought from my mind because I knew it was unfair to Penelope to think about somebody else, especially since she was going to be my wife and the mother of my child. I expected everything to be the same as before she left. She apologized to me often about what happened, and I always told her she was forgiven. It didn't matter anymore.

But as the days went by, I realized that our conversations at dinner were forced, like she didn't feel like talking most of the time. She also quit her job even though she was only five weeks pregnant. She loved her job, so I was surprised that she left it so suddenly.

It was evident that we didn't have anything in common anymore. Penelope didn't like sports, playing them or watching them, and we didn't have the same taste in movies, music, or television. Most of the time, we had nothing to talk about and I wasn't sure why. Was it always like this? Was I just so blind and infatuated by her beauty that I hadn't noticed it before?

The sex was mediocre and passionless. When I questioned Penelope about it, she said the hormones from the pregnancy were making her moody. I dropped the topic and hoped that she was telling the truth. Since my bedroom needs weren't being met, I assumed she would compensate in other ways, by going down on me or doing other things, but she never made an effort. I didn't want to tell her what I wanted. I wanted her to do it on her own.

The humongous ring was always on her finger everywhere she went, which made me happy that she was proud of her commitment to me. She was also mesmerized by the ring I bought her, which had over two-karats of diamonds in the band, and had cost me a fortune. When we walked around the park after work, we walked hand in hand, but nothing was said. I tried to strike up a conversation with her or tell her a joke, but she never seemed to understand what I was saying. Sometimes I wondered if she was listening to me at all.

I told Brian about my engagement to Penelope, and like everyone else in the office, he was stunned by the news. He couldn't believe I would dump Scarlet after I confessed how much I loved her, but I had to remind him that a baby was involved. He never understood the relevance.

When I came home from work one night, Penelope was cooking in the kitchen, preparing dinner like she did every night. I put down my bag and I realized that she didn't ask me how my day was. In fact, she *never* asked me how my day was. When I really thought about it, Penelope didn't speak to me very often, and when she did, it was usually in response to something I said.

I stared at her back as she moved in the kitchen and I felt the fear take hold. Perhaps Penelope didn't really love me and never had. I understood that we were doing this just for the baby, but I expected us both to make an effort on our romantic relationship. It dawned on me that our relationship had always been this way; empty, lifeless, and dull, but I didn't understand why I didn't notice it before. Why was I only realizing it now?

When I walked over to Penelope, she didn't turn around even though she knew I was right behind her. I wrapped my arms around her waist and kissed her cheek, but she still didn't turn around as she continued to focus on the stove. She cared more about dinner than embracing her fiancé after he got home from work. She didn't even say hi to me. It was like we weren't even friends. How were we supposed to be loving parents to our kid if we didn't even respect each other? She told me how much she loved me, but now she was indifferent to my existence. I didn't understand what was going on.

"How was your day?" I asked.

"It was okay," she said with a sigh. She stirred the rice in the pan then checked the chicken in the oven. Patiently, I waited for her to turn around and acknowledge me, ask me about my day, kiss me on the cheek, or even look at me. It was obviously a lost cause.

I sat on the couch and stared at the blank television screen, wishing that this wasn't happening to me. My choice could never be changed. I was stuck with the decision I made, one that I regretted. What was the point of marrying a woman who didn't even like me? My kid would see through that eventually. That his mother and father didn't love each other. That's not what I wanted at all. I wanted to be a real family—not a broken one.

My phone rang from my pocket and I pulled it out, not caring about who it was. There was only one person that I wanted to talk to, and I knew she would never contact me. I'd lost her forever. The screen displayed Ryan's name and I took a deep breath, knowing that this conversation was going to be painful. I walked into my bedroom and shut the door before I answered it.

"Hello?"

Even though Ryan didn't yell, I could tell how angry he was by his words. "I'm not calling to discuss what the fuck you did to my sister," he snapped. "I just want to know what's going on with the will. We are running out of time."

"I'm working on it," I said. "I'm going as fast as I can."

"Well, it isn't good enough, but then again, I shouldn't be surprised." Ryan hung up the phone and I listened to the line go dead. I was shocked that the conversation hadn't been worse.

"Dinner is ready," Penelope called from the kitchen. I dropped the phone in my pocket and walked into the dining room. Penelope sat across from me while we ate. I said nothing as I ate my chicken and rice, which was delicious, as I waited for Penelope to speak up first. For the entire length of the meal, she didn't speak or look at me, even though dinnertime was the hour you were supposed to spend talking with your family about your day. In our case, it was just awkward.

She grabbed the dishes from the table then washed and placed them in the dishwasher. I didn't move from my spot at the table. I just stared at the wall straight ahead, which had no ornamentation or decoration at all. Penelope moved to the couch and started watching an annoying reality show. She didn't even notice me sitting in the chair staring straight ahead.

When I got in the shower, I started crying, letting myself fall apart under the protection of the falling water. For an hour, I sat in the shower and cried like a pathetic little girl, realizing that I'd made the biggest mistake of my life. I needed Scarlet, but she would never be mine again and I didn't blame her. The water fell on my body until my skin was pruned, but I couldn't move away. I couldn't accept the truth. I'd lost the most important thing in my life and could never get it back. I traded in a stallion for a mule. The worst part was I knew how much pain I caused Scarlet. The memory of her tears made me hate myself more than I already did. I was nothing but a monster destined to betray her over and over. I wanted to do the right thing for my child, but I realized it was the wrong decision. Now my kid would have to live with a depressed dad. If I was with Scarlet, he would have a wonderful stepmother that would love him more than this own mother did. My life had become dead and meaningless, and it wasn't until I started a relationship with Scarlet, started really living, that I realized how empty my life was. My life with Penelope had always been this way, but now that I was in love with Scarlet, I realized I didn't belong with her anymore. I belonged with Scarlet.

10

I slept on the couch that night and Penelope didn't ask why. She probably didn't even notice I was gone. When I went to work in the morning, I didn't speak to anyone or acknowledge a single person. My secretary said hello to me, but I passed by her without saying a word.

My office door suddenly opened, but I was so indifferent to everything that I didn't care at all. My life had no purpose or meaning. I was in a relationship that was dead and lifeless, with a woman that didn't care if I lived or died. Finally, I looked up at the person who entered my office unannounced. It was Brian.

"I have to talk to you," he said quickly. "I tried calling you last night, but you didn't answer."

I shrugged. "I don't remember where I put my phone."

Brian stared at me for a moment, but then continued on. "It's about Penelope."

"What about her?" I said with an indifferent voice. "You still want to know what she's like in the sack?" I asked. "Well, she sucks—there you go."

"What the hell is wrong with you?" he asked. "Are you drunk?"

"Maybe." I sighed.

"Are you high?"

I shrugged.

Brian shook his head. "Anyway, I have to tell you something."

"You already said that."

"My friend that works on Wall Street with Christian—"

"Who's Christian?"

"The guy Penelope cheated on you with."

"Oh, him." I sighed.

Brian stared at me again. "He told me that he knocked up Penelope, but he didn't want her anymore since she was pregnant. He dumped her and kicked her out. She lost her job because she was so depressed."

I rose from behind my desk, shaking in anger. "What did you say?"

Brian sighed. "I'm not making this up," he said. "She told you the baby was yours because she had nowhere else to go. I'm sorry, man."

The anger inside my body ignited like a lit stick of dynamite. It was one thing to leave Scarlet because I was accepting my responsibilities as a father, doing the right thing for my kid, but knowing that I left the love of my life because Penelope lied to me made me snap. I grabbed my bag and stormed out of the office with Brian following behind me.

"Where are you going?" he asked.

"I'm calling in sick," I said as I strode out of the office. Instead of the elevator, I took the stairs two at a time, and practically ran through the lobby. I yelled down a cab, and when it pulled up in front of my apartment, I threw a fifty at the driver and ran up the stairs to my apartment.

The door slammed open and Penelope jumped from the couch, frightened of the way I stormed in. My bag fell to the floor, and I kicked the door shut behind me. Never in my life had I hit a woman or even thought about it, but I could've done it right then. I could've beat the shit out of her.

"Why are you home so early?" she asked quietly.

I moved closer to her, and she inched away from me. It was obvious how frightened she was of me. She was smart. If she knew what I wanted to do to her, she would have been running for cover.

"Sean?"

"I could kill you, Penelope. I SWEAR TO FUCKING GOD, I COULD KILL YOU!"

Penelope practically ran to the other side of the room, but I chased her down and pinned her against the wall. She tried to move away, but I held her by her shoulders. "Please don't hurt me," she begged.

"We'll see," I spat. "So that bastard isn't mine, and you made me believe that it was? You are the fucking devil, Penelope. I can't believe you would do this to me. I was happy with Scarlet, but you tricked me into being with you. Do you understand that you ruined my life? Do you get that?" I shook her shoulders and she started to cry. "I have no sympathy for you." I released my hold on her and stood back, not because I felt bad for scaring her, but because I knew I was going to hurt her. "Scarlet is everything to me and now I lost her—she's *gone*."

Penelope lowered her gaze to the floor, and I wanted to punch her in the face. Instead, I grabbed her stuff and started shoving it into boxes then I threw them out into the hallway. Penelope cried as she watched me throw her belongings outside of the apartment, breaking some of her things when they collided with the ground.

"Please stop, Sean."

"Get the fuck out of my apartment!" I threw her clothes in the hallway, not bothering to put them in boxes anymore. "Get out."

"Sean," she cried. "Listen to me."

"NO!"

After all her shit was out of the apartment, I grabbed her arm and dragged her from the room and into the hallway.

"I have nowhere else to go," she cried. "Please, Sean. I lost my job and I have no one to turn to. Please don't kick me out."

"Fuck off."

I slammed the door in her face and locked the bolt. Her cries could be heard through the doorway and I listened to the sounds for a while. Last week, I was the happiest guy on the planet, and now I was the most miserable person in history. Scarlet was gone forever. I could try to win her back, but she would never take me—not after I betrayed her twice. She would be stupid if she even considered it. My life was empty and I had no meaning—I was dead.

Penelope continued to cry in the hallway, and I was irritated by the noise. The woman lied about everything, but I knew she was finally telling the truth. She really had nowhere else to go. Her parents had died years ago and she was an only child. She had no friends because she was a bitch, and no other ex-boyfriends that were stupid enough to take her back. After I took a deep breath, I opened the door and started to carry her stuff back into the apartment. Penelope was sitting against the wall and she stopped crying when she saw me carry everything back into the living room.

Penelope got to her feet and came back inside, and I shut the door behind her.

"Thank you so much," she said as she wiped away her tears. "I really have no one else."

"You can stay here for a month. After that, I'm kicking you out. You are staying on the couch. And don't look at me or speak to me for any reason—which shouldn't be difficult for you."

She watched me walk away and open the cabinet. I grabbed as much hard liquor as I could, and I carried it into my bedroom. I returned to the kitchen and grabbed all the old vicodin that I could find. Then I went into my bedroom and slammed the door behind me, leaving Penelope alone in the living room.

I was being stupid and reckless, but I didn't care. Never in my life had I been in so much pain. I opened the bottle and chugged the rum, but when the pain didn't go away, I popped a vicodin pill and felt my mind begin to blur. It wasn't a solution to my problem, but then again, no solution existed. All I had was the alcohol and the left over pills. I wasn't going to work and I wasn't leaving my apartment. The alcohol would kill me or the drugs would. It didn't matter which.

11

Scarlet

Ryan left for work in the morning, but I decided to stay home and work on editing a manuscript that I was almost finished with. Sean was always on my mind, but I didn't let myself fall to a depression. I had to pretend that I was okay, hoping that someday I actually would be. Now that I had a purpose, supporting both Ryan and myself, I knew I couldn't fall prey to the darker emotions that were growing inside me. Sean's betrayal did more than just break my heart. It killed my soul.

The sound of a knock on the door made me flinch. Cortland was at work and so was Ryan. Only one other person would come visit me and he wasn't welcome. If Sean was at the door, I would punch him without thinking twice. When I looked through the peephole, I gasped.

"Janice?" I asked when I opened the door.

She smiled and immediately hugged me, holding onto me for a moment. I returned her embrace and instantly noted the weight she had lost. She was much thinner than she had ever been. I pulled away.

"What are you doing here?" I asked as I shut the door behind her.

"I came to see you," she said. "You won't return my phone calls, so I had to resort to this. I apologize for barging in on your life."

"It's okay," I said. "Can I get you something? Maybe some ice cream?"

Janice's cheeks reddened. "I've lost some weight, as you can tell."

"What's going on?"

"Can I start by saying how sorry I am about what happened with Sean? I never would have done that if I knew how you felt about him—you have to believe me. You're my best friend. You know I would never hurt you like that."

I sighed. "I should be apologizing to you. You did nothing wrong, Janice. I should have called you and told you where I was and what I was thinking. It was wrong for me to leave you in the dark like that. Do you forgive me?"

"Of course," she said as she hugged me. "I'm so glad that we worked this out. I was so worried about you."

"I'm okay, Janice. You are the one that we should worry about." I looked at her body. "You are practically anorexic."

Janice sighed. "Now that we're friends again, there is something I need to tell you."

I took Janice's hand and pulled into the living room. "Go ahead," I said.

"After Sean came to R and R—"

"When did Sean come to R and R?" I asked. "What are you talking about?"

"He didn't tell you?" she asked.

"No," I said.

"Well, Sean came looking for you after you left. He asked me if I knew anything, and I said I didn't. I tried calling you, but you didn't answer. Carl took him into his office. Minutes later, Sean was punching Carl in the face, beating the shit out of him right in his own office. By the time Sean ran away, Carl was unconscious. An ambulance took him to the hospital. He was in a coma for three days because of the swelling to his brain."

"Oh my god," I said as I covered my face. "I can't believe Sean did that."

"He probably didn't tell you because he knew how mad you would be."

"They never found out it was Sean?"

"No," she said. "Carl questioned me when he came back to work, but I denied any knowledge of him, and said I had never seen him before. That's when the assaults began."

I stared at Janice. "Carl came after you?"

She nodded and averted her gaze. "As punishment for hiding Sean's identity."

I shook my head. "I'm so sorry, Janice. This is all my fault. If I had stood up to Carl, this never would have happened."

"Don't blame yourself," she said. "Please don't do that."

"Is that why you're here? Are you running from him?"

"No," she said. "But I had to tell someone. I have no one to turn to. All the girls in the office turn a blind eye because they don't want to be the next victim. You and I were the last girls in

106

the office he hadn't propositioned, so after you left the company, I was next."

"We have to do something."

"But what?" she asked.

"I don't know," I said. "But this is bullshit. He can't treat us like this. I'm glad Sean beat the shit out of him."

"I am too." She smiled. "Are you two still together?"

"No," I said quickly.

"Last time I talked to him, he told me that he loved you."

"Well, he left me because Penelope wanted him back—she's having his baby."

Janice grabbed my hand and squeezed it. "I'm sorry, Scarlet. I had no idea."

"It's okay," I whispered.

The front door opened and Ryan and Cortland came inside. They both stopped when they saw Janice sitting in the living room. They stared at her for moment, particularly Ryan, and then finally came into the sitting area.

"This is Janice," I said to them. They approached us on the couch and I turned to her. "Janice, this is my brother, Ryan."

Janice stared at him with a smile on her lips. Her cheeks were slightly red. They shook hands and Janice said, "I'm normally not this skinny."

Ryan nodded with a smile. "Okay. Good to know."

Then, I introduced her to Cortland. The men sat on the other couch and looked at us.

"What's going on?" Ryan asked. "I didn't know you had any friends."

I rolled my eyes. "I used to work at R and R with her. Apparently, our boss is assaulting her now. We are trying to figure out a way to bring him down."

"It's impossible." Janice sighed.

"No," I said. "We are going to do this. I was a coward before, but I'm not anymore. We are going to fight this time. This piece of shit is going down."

"Can we help?" Cortland asked.

"I don't know," I said. "We need proof that he is sexually harassing her at work."

"Aren't there cameras in the building?" Cortland asked.

"No," I said. "Not in our office."

Cortland shook his head. "This pervert covers his ass," he said. He thought for a moment. "What if we catch him in the act? I'll bring my camera and record your boss in action then we'll upload it to their server so it will infect their entire network and everyone will see it. This guy won't get off with a warning—he'll be fired."

My lips stretched into a smile. "That a great idea!" I said. I got up and hugged Cortland tightly. "You'll help us?"

"Of course," he said. "Ryan and I both can."

Ryan cleared his throat. "Well, in order for this to work, we are going to need bait. Since Scarlet doesn't work there anymore, Janice will have to do it." He turned to her. "Are you comfortable with that?"

Janice thought for a moment. "Will I have to go through with it—all the way?" she asked apprehensively.

"We would never let that happen," Ryan said quickly. "This is what we'll do. Cortland will hide and videotape the whole thing. Scarlet will get me into the building and I'll hide around the corner. When he starts his attack, I'll come in and stop him so Cortland can get the entire interaction. We'll show him assaulting you while you continue to say no. There will be no room for misinterpretation. The cops will even be involved, especially if the other girls come forward and admit the truth—that he assaulted them too."

"Then I'll upload it the next morning on their servers," Cortland said. "The fucker will be sitting at his desk when I upload the whole video, watching it with a look of horror on his face."

The plan sounded feasible. I realized it was actually going to happen. Retribution was coming our way. I grabbed Janice's hand and she started crying. I felt my own tears fall at the sight, knowing how much pain Carl had caused both of us. I hugged her and held her tightly, rocking her back and forth. "We are going to get him," I whispered.

"I know," she said. "I'm so happy." She turned to Cortland and Ryan. "Thank you so much."

Ryan stared at her. "Of course," he said.

Cortland nodded. "It's the right thing to do," he said. "When do we leave?"

"My plane leaves tomorrow," Janice said.

I turned to Cortland. "Can you get the time off?"

"It shouldn't be a problem," he said.

"Good," I said.

"I can't believe we are actually doing this," Janice said.

"It's been a long time coming," I said.

I opened my laptop and bought the tickets online for Ryan and I. Cortland paid for his own ticket and Janice already had her return flight booked for early the next morning.

Ryan shifted his weight on the couch. "Would you like to go out to dinner?" Ryan asked us. He was looking at Janice, but I knew he was addressing me as well.

"You must be hungry," I said to Janice. "The food in coach sucks."

"Yes, I'm starving."

We rose from the living room and walked out the door then made it to the street. Cortland drove us to Pike's Market, and we went to the Italian restaurant that Cortland and I had visited a few weeks earlier. Cortland sat directly across from me and Janice sat across from Ryan.

Cortland and I shared glances, silently communicating with each other. Ryan kept starting at Janice, but then he would look away when she noticed his stare. They continued to sneak glances at each other. They were acting like they were in high school. I knew Janice was very forward when she had a love interest, but she was being shy. I wondered if it was because she really liked

Ryan, or if it was because he was my brother.

"So, are you seeing anybody?" I asked Janice.

She smiled at me. "No."

I nodded. "Cortland has a girlfriend—she's Brazilian." That was my way of saying Cortland was off limits, leaving Ryan for the taking.

She laughed. "That's interesting."

"Ryan owns a tattoo shop," I said. I knew I was doing most of the talking for my brother because he was being particularly quiet, not his normal self at all. I assumed that meant he really liked Janice, even though they'd just met.

"But it doesn't look like you have any tattoos," she said as she looked at Ryan's arms.

Ryan smiled. "Well—I—yeah just don't really—want one," he mumbled incoherently. "Yeah."

Cortland covered his face while he laughed and I tried to swallow my giggles. My brother was making an idiot out of himself. He wasn't the charming stud that he usually was with girls.

"That's cool," she said apprehensively.

I tried to break the awkward moment. "When I came to Seattle, my brother took care of me. He let me live with him rent free and even gave me an allowance. He's very sweet."

"That was so nice of you." Janice smiled at him. "I wish I had a brother like that."

Ryan cleared his throat and didn't look at her. "Thanks," he said. He looked down at his menu and ignored her stare.

I covered my face with my hands, embarrassed for my brother. "He normally isn't like this," I whispered to her. "He's just nervous around you for some reason."

"I think it's cute," she said loudly.

Ryan's cheeks turned red and he continued to look down, avoiding her look.

"Anyway," I said, more embarrassed by my brother with every passing second. "So how are things with you? Other than the nightmare at work?"

Janice laughed. "It's okay," she said. "I've missed you a lot, Scarlet. The truth is I've been pretty miserable without you."

"I missed you, too." I smiled.

"Promise me you won't ignore me like that again," she said. "Even if I really piss you off."

"Okay." I laughed. "I'll yell at you next time."

"What did you do?" Cortland asked.

I spoke before Janice could answer. "She borrowed one of my outfits and never returned it." Since Ryan was interested in Janice, I didn't want him to know she'd slept with Sean. It wasn't a fair first impression.

Cortland raised his eyebrow for a moment, confused that I would cut out a friend over something so petty, but then he nodded and didn't comment.

After we finished our dinner, Cortland tried to pay for the whole check, but Ryan convinced him to split it with him.

Normally, I would just pay for our meal, but since Janice was there, I let Ryan do the check dance.

When we got back to the apartment, Ryan went into his room then came out a few moments later. "I changed the sheets and got the bed ready," he said. "You are welcome to sleep in my room."

Janice smiled. "I don't mind sleeping on the couch."

"I insist." He smiled.

"Okay," she said after a moment. Her cheeks were turning red as she looked at him. Janice and I went into my room, and I gave her a change of clothes to wear.

"Can I ask you something?" Janice said.

"Sure," I said. "What is it?"

"Would it bother you if I asked out Ryan? I know he's your brother, so I don't want to make you upset or uncomfortable. If I am crossing a line, just say so."

I smiled. "He's all yours," I said. "It doesn't bother me in the least."

"Really?" she asked happily.

"Really. I can't imagine him dating anyone better."

She smiled. "That's sweet." Janice left the bedroom and closed the door behind her. I wondered if she would go into the living room and start talking to Ryan. Hopefully, he wouldn't make such an idiot of himself when no one was around. I loved the idea of Janice and Ryan together. I was worried that he would never find anyone. If things worked out, Ryan would be happy with a partner and I would still be single. I would die alone.

12

The next morning, we grabbed all our gear and headed to the airport. We traveled light since we knew we would only be there for a quick trip. I brought one bag with me, with just two outfits. Janice and Ryan were more talkative than they were the night before, and I suspected something had happened between them after I went to bed. Janice didn't say anything and I didn't press her on the subject.

When we got on the plane, I sat next to Cortland on purpose so Janice and Ryan would have to sit together in a different row.

"We are so sneaky," Cortland said.

"I know." I smiled. "Has he said anything to you?"

"Just that he likes Janice—that's about it."

"Did he say why? He just met her."

Cortland shook his head. "He said sometimes you just know. It's like an instant chemistry. He's totally smitten with her."

"I've never seen him act this way," I said. "He sounded so stupid yesterday."

Cortland laughed. "I know," he said. "That was hilarious."

"Well, Janice must think he's cute because she said she wanted to go out with him."

"Poor girl," Cortland said as he shook his head. "She

doesn't know what she's getting into."

"I hope it works out," I said. "I want Ryan to be happy with someone."

"We'll keep our fingers crossed," he said. He leaned back in his chair as the plane took off. Soon we were gliding at a higher altitude. "Are you worried about seeing Sean?" he asked.

"Why would I see him?"

"He lives in New York, right?"

"Have you been to Manhattan?"

"No."

I rolled my eyes. "Seven million people live in the city alone—I'm not going to bump into him."

Cortland nodded his head. "Well, I hope I run into him."

I smiled. "I'm fine, Cortland. He isn't worth it."

"Has he tried contacting you?"

"No," I said. "And I doubt he ever will. He has what he's always wanted."

"He'll realize he made the wrong choice—I promise you."

"Even though Sean betrayed me again, I don't want him to regret his choice. I want him to be happy—even if it isn't with me."

"You sound like you're over him."

I put down the magazine I was reading and looked at him. "If I tell you something, you promise you won't tell Ryan?"

"As long as it doesn't jeopardize your safety," he said.

I rolled my eyes. "I'm not over Sean and I never will be.

His betrayal almost killed me, and I've spent every night crying myself to sleep. He was the one, Cortland—the *one*. I don't expect that I'll ever date again, let alone love somebody."

"So you were lying before?"

I nodded. "I wanted to protect Ryan. It hurts him to see me in pain."

"It hurts me too," he said.

"But not in the same way," I said. "I'm never going to be fine, but this is the closest I've been to it in a while. I'm glad we are taking down my boss—he deserves it."

"I am too," he said. "It looks like you tied up all your threads. You are standing up to your boss, you are back to normal with Janice, and you gave Sean a second chance even though that went to waste. Now you are a stronger person."

"I suppose." I took a deep breath and closed my eyes.

"What's wrong?"

"I just wish that I had Sean." I sighed. "I've never been so happy in my whole life."

"You'll find it again someday," he said as he held my hand. He lifted it to his lips and kissed my knuckles. "It's going to be okay."

"I hope so." I looked away and watched my brother. He was smiling while talking to Janice, and I knew it was going well. It was a six-hour flight to New York—that was plenty of time to connect.

When we arrived in New York, we took a taxi to Janice's

apartment up town. The place was small with limited space, but we managed to squeeze in. Cortland and Ryan would sleep on the floor in the living room while I slept on the couch. Cortland prepared all his equipment and set the camera to transmit the live feed to his computer, just in case Carl caught us and broke the camera.

"What should we do tonight?" Cortland asked while we all sat in the living room. Janice walked into her bedroom and disappeared "We should go out since we are in the city."

I nodded. "Janice and I can show you guys around," I said. "Do you want to go out for drinks?"

"Sure," Janice said.

"It can be a double date," Cortland said.

I looked at him. "What do you mean?"

"Since I have a girlfriend back at home, I'm not available, and I'm assuming that you aren't interested in mingling either."

"Yes."

"Then we can be a couple for the night—it makes sense."

Ryan stared at us, but didn't seem bothered by Cortland's suggestion. "Okay," I agreed.

"Good," he said. "It's hard to keep the ladies away."

"Great." I sighed. "My date is conceited."

He laughed. "I'm just saying," he said. "I know Monnique would prefer this arrangement."

"I'm assuming you haven't told her that we slept together?" I asked.

Cortland shook his head. "No," he said. "I don't think it matters."

"And you were giving me grief about Sean?" I laughed.

"I realized you were right. Sean would have been uncomfortable around me and I don't want Monnique to feel threatened by you."

Janice emerged from her room and checked her hair in the mirror. Ryan blatantly watched her as she appraised herself in the mirror.

"Well, let's go," she said.

The four of us left the apartment and walked towards a bar a few blocks away. Cortland and Ryan stared at the lights of the city, admiring the tall skyscrapers and the people walking by. The sidewalk was crowded with tourists, so it took us a while to finally get inside the bar.

We sat in the corner where there were two wide sofas facing each other. Cortland and I sat together and Ryan and Janice sat on the opposite couch facing us. Ryan placed his hands on his thigh in an awkward position, and Janice left her hand resting on her lap, close to his. They still seemed self-conscious around each other, but Ryan was a lot more talkative than before. It was obvious that he felt more comfortable with Janice.

Cortland placed his arm around my shoulders but the closeness didn't bother me. The nature of our relationship was platonic, and since we'd already slept together, I didn't feel uncomfortable when he touched me. Ryan glared at Cortland, but

Cortland didn't pull his arm away. He made it clear that this was a relationship of convenience.

"Is that really necessary?" Ryan asked.

Cortland nodded. "Scarlet is a gorgeous woman," he said. "There are three men staring at her right now, and another woman is staring at me. I'm just making it clear that I'm not available."

Ryan continued to stare at Cortland. "Don't push me."

"You're overreacting, Ryan," I said.

"What's going on?" Janice asked.

"Cortland and I slept together and now we are just friends," I explained. "Ryan is still mad about it even though nothing will happen between us again."

"It better not," Ryan said.

"It won't," Cortland said.

Janice turned to Ryan. "I think it's cute that you are so protective of your sister."

Ryan smiled. "She is everything to me—when she isn't being a brat, at least."

Janice laughed. "Yes, Scarlet can be a pain in the ass at times."

"Not you too." I sighed.

The waitress brought our drinks and we sipped our beverages. Janice and I both had wine while the men ordered brandy and scotch. We conversed for a few hours until I started to feel my eyes sag from exhaustion. The plane ride was six hours long and it made me lethargic and lifeless. Cortland noticed how tired I was.

"Are you ready to go?" he asked. "I'm tired too."

I nodded. "Are you guys staying out?" I asked Ryan.

Ryan turned to Janice. "Can I take you to dinner?"

"That sounds great." Janice smiled.

We all stood up and Ryan pulled Cortland aside. It was obvious by the way he grabbed Cortland's arm that he was threatening him. I knew it had something to do with me.

I turned to Janice. "Do you like him?"

Janice smiled and averted her gaze. "Since he's your brother, this is kind of awkward."

I rolled my eyes. "My brother and I are really open about our personal life. What you don't tell me, he will later. I really don't mind—it doesn't bother me."

"Well, Ryan is—hot—I mean, really handsome." She smiled. "Why didn't you tell me your brother was such a catch?"

I laughed. "I guess because I don't see him like that."

"You never even mentioned that you had a brother."

The comment made me feel guilty. Ryan and I hardly spoke for an entire year. "I know." I sighed. "But we are very close now."

"He's such a sweet guy," she said. "Last night we started talking about his artwork and his dreams—he's amazing." I smiled as I listened to her. Ryan deserved to be with someone who thought he was nothing less than perfect. I wanted Ryan to have the love I had with Sean—but with a better person. "And—we kissed—for a while. Scarlet, he is an amazing kisser. I can tell he knows what he's doing—in other ways."

I decided not to comment on that last part. Ryan was open about his personal life and I knew he had a lot of sexual partners—*a lot*. Even though Janice wasn't exactly a prude, I was afraid his scandalous lifestyle would chase her away. I decided it was best if he told her, not me. "Ryan is a great guy—one of the best I know."

Janice smiled. "I really like him, Scarlet."

"I'm glad."

Ryan came back over to us and he stared at me. I took that as my cue to leave him alone with Janice. Cortland was waiting for me on the other side of the room, so I headed over to him and we left the bar, walking back to the apartment. When we got to Janice's door, I took out her spare key and opened the lock.

"What did Ryan say?" I asked.

"That if we fuck, he's going to kill me."

I rolled my eyes. "Talk about being psycho," I said. "It's really none of his business if we did."

Cortland pulled out the inflatable mattress that Janice had taken out of the closet. "It bothers me that he doesn't trust me. I thought he forgave me for that whole thing—apparently not."

"Don't worry about him," I said as I took out a change of clothes from my pack. "He's just upset about what Sean did to me. I know he has been waiting for me to snap and spiral out of control. He's just concerned for me—that's all. We are away from home and in a romantic city. If we decided to sleep together, no one would ever know."

Cortland sighed. "I'm not that type of guy—not anymore, at least."

I walked over to Cortland and kissed him on the cheek. "I know," I said. "Don't let Ryan get under your skin. He is just worried—that's all." I walked into the bathroom and changed my clothes, slipping into some pink pajamas. Cortland was already changed by the time I came out of the room.

Cortland moved the mattress next to the couch, so we would be close together while we slept. I turned off all the lights and settled on the couch with the blankets over my body. Cortland was lying below me, close enough that I could hear him breathe.

"Are you scared?" he asked.

"About what?"

"To take down your old boss?"

I shook my head. "No," I said. "I'm ready for this. I should have done this a long time ago. If I wasn't such a coward and took off from New York, I could have done something and Janice wouldn't be dealing with this at all."

Cortland reached up and grabbed my hand. "You are here now—that's all that matters."

I smiled at him even though he couldn't see me. "Thanks."

We lay in silence for a long time and said nothing. I couldn't fall asleep and I knew Cortland couldn't either by the sound of his breathing. Hours went by and I never closed my eyes. Sometime in the middle of the night, I heard the front door open and Ryan and Janice crept into the room, silently maneuvering around the furniture. Ryan had a bed made for him next to Cortland, but they both walked into Janice's room. The door closed behind them and I heard the lock click.

"Ryan is going to score," Cortland whispered. I could hear the smile in his voice. "Is Janice easy?"

"She has slept around before," I said. "But I know she really likes Ryan. I don't think this is a one-night stand."

"Hopefully, we don't have to listen to it," he said.

"Ryan is really loud—at least at home."

"That's awkward." Cortland laughed.

"You're telling me," I said sarcastically.

A few minutes later, I could hear Janice moaning. The muffled sound of her cries made me realize she was trying to be quiet, but was having a difficult time.

"Is she faking it?" Cortland asked.

"I don't know what her normal sex noises are." I laughed.

"Well, I know girls are pros at that."

Janice's moans became louder and it was too distracting not to notice. Cortland and I just lay there together and listened, awkwardly.

"Well, it sounds like Ryan is doing a good job," Cortland said.

"That is so awkward." I laughed.

"We were both thinking it." He laughed. "I don't get why he can fuck around with your friend, but it's just horrifying if I

124

date you."

"You misunderstood him," I said. "Ryan would be ecstatic if you and I got together."

"He told you that?"

"No," I said. "But I can tell. It just bothers him if you are using me."

"Well, he is using Janice," he said. "He lives on the other side of the country. This obviously isn't going to go anywhere."

"I don't think he's using her. I can tell he really likes her."

Cortland sighed. "Then he's setting himself up for heartbreak. They just met—she's not going to move for him. And Ryan can't leave Seattle—he's got you and the shop."

"You're right," I said. "Why does Ryan finally like someone that he can't have?"

"It always works out that way."

I turned on my side and closed my eyes. The sound of their love making stopped and I finally felt relaxed enough to fall asleep. Cortland said something, but I wasn't listening. I was already asleep.

13

The next morning, Ryan and Janice walked out of her bedroom, dressed and ready for the day. Janice was wearing a tight dress that made her look slim and beautiful. The earrings she wore highlighted her eyes and made her look glamorous.

"You look hot," I said.

She smiled. "Got to make sure Carl can't resist."

"Well, that definitely won't be a problem."

Ryan poured a cup of coffee then handed it to her. He kissed her on the head before he made his own and drank it black. I'd never seen Ryan so attentive to a woman before. When that other girl came to the apartment, Ryan blatantly ignored her until she left. With Janice, Ryan was a whole new man, tender and gentle. Cortland caught the exchange from his seat at the kitchen table.

"Did you have fun last night?" Cortland smiled.

Ryan smiled and Janice blushed. "A lot of fun," Ryan answered.

I fixed my hair in the mirror then turned to them. "Let's go," I said.

Janice sighed and placed her purse over her arm. It was obvious that she was nervous and frightened about the plan. I didn't blame her. We left her apartment and took a cab to the front of R and R. We stopped when we were outside the doors.

I looked at my brother. "You can't hurt him, Ryan. Just pull him off and keep Janice safe—that's it."

"As much as I enjoyed Sean beating the shit of him, I don't want you to get in trouble for assault either," Janice said to Ryan.

Cortland raised an eyebrow. "Sean attacked your boss?"

"What is she talking about, Scar?" Ryan asked.

I sighed. "Long story short, when Sean found out what that creep did to me, he beat Carl up in his own office and sent him to the hospital for a week. Sean didn't tell me anything—Janice did."

"Sean just snapped—he was livid," Janice said.

Ryan said nothing for a moment. "Well, I respect him for that, despite what he did to you, Scar."

Cortland nodded. "Me too."

"It doesn't matter," I said. I turned to Janice. "Are you nervous?"

"Yes," Janice said. "I'm scared."

"My brother would never let anything happen to you."

"I know," she said.

"Let's get this mother fucker," I said as I walked into the building. Because it was the weekend, the lobby was deserted, and we had no trouble getting into the elevator and to the twentieth floor. When we stepped out of the elevator, Janice checked to make sure the office was empty before she ushered us in. Cortland made a hole in the wall of the cubicle that was across from Janice's desk and had the camera ready for Carl to make his move. Ryan and I hid in a cubicle on the other side of the room so we could hear everything without being seen.

Ryan was breathing heavily next to me. I knew he was angry that this was happening to Janice and had already happened to me. The relationship between him and Janice was still in a gray area, but I could tell that he cared about her in a profound way. She wasn't just a fuck-buddy. Ryan would never hurt my best friend and make it awkward between us, despite the fact that I had done it to him when I slept with Cortland. Even though I hurt Ryan more than once, he would never betray me in any way. I didn't deserve his love.

Janice was typing on the keyboard, working like any other day, when I heard the sound of heavy footsteps thud down the hall. Without looking, I knew it was Carl by the shuffle of his lazy feet.

"You are here late," I heard Carl say to Janice in a sleazy voice. It sounded like he was trying to be flirtatious but he was failing miserably. Ryan locked his gaze to mine and I nodded, silently confirming Carl's voice. Ryan clenched his fists together and his veins popped on his hands.

"I like a woman who works hard for her money," Carl said as he stepped closer to her. The anger rushed through my body at his words. I had heard him say those very words to me on countless occasions. The fucker was too lazy to come up with new lines. "You look beautiful this evening."

"Thank you," Janice said calmly. "I'm just finishing my work and I'll be out of your way."

"I don't want you to leave," he snapped. His voice turned suddenly cold and hard, like he was trying to control her with his words alone. "I think you have another responsibility that you're forgetting."

The sound of a belt coming loose could he heard as it dropped to the floor. Ryan tried to sit up, but I steadied him. "Not yet," I said. "She'll be fine."

"I love working here, Mr. Rogers, but I feel uncomfortable by the sexual advances that you continue to make at me and the rest of the staff. Please let me finish my work. I already said I'm not interested."

Janice kept her voice calm and strong, and I was mesmerized by her strength. I would have already been crying at that point. The sound of a struggle could be heard and I knew Carl was advancing on her. Ryan tried to get up again, but I held him back.

"Wait," I said.

"Stop it," she screamed. "You're hurting me! I said get off of me!"

I released Ryan's arm and he bolted from the cubicle, running down the walkway as he charged Carl. I stood up and looked over the wall as Ryan grabbed him and kneed him right in the testicles.

"Get off of her!" he said as pushed Carl.

Carl was on the ground with his knees to his chest and his dick still hanging out. He started moaning in pain. Ryan turned to

Janice and grabbed her arm. "Are you okay?"

She nodded, too frightened to speak.

"Let's go," he said.

Ryan and Janice walked away and I followed behind them. Cortland emerged from the office a moment later and we left the building quickly. I was certain Carl hadn't seen us because he was still paralyzed by the pain in his groin. We jumped into a cab and returned to the apartment.

"Did you get it?" I asked Cortland when we walked into the living room.

"Yes." He smiled. "I got the whole thing. The audio came out perfectly. I can hear every word they said. Cortland opened his computer and sat on the couch, watching the video again. I sat next to him and smiled when I saw the footage. It was perfect.

The sound of Janice sniffing caught my attention. I looked up to see Ryan cupping her cheek as he kissed her tears away. He grabbed her face and kissed her gently, and I was moved by his affection. It reminded me of Sean. When I realized I was intruding on their privacy, I looked away. Ryan's gentle touch amazed me. I had never seen him that way with anyone—ever. Now that I knew they were serious, I wasn't sure what it would mean for their relationship because they lived three thousand miles apart.

14

The next morning, we took a cab to the office and stood outside for a moment. Ryan was holding Janice and whispering to her, and Cortland and I were standing beside them awkwardly, waiting for them to finish their goodbye. It was obvious that Ryan was in love with Janice. I could hear it through her bedroom wall.

"He won't touch you," Ryan said to her. "There will be too many people around."

She nodded. "You're right."

"And if he does, I'll kill him." He smiled. "Then the problem will be solved."

She smiled. "Okay."

Ryan kissed her for a long moment then pulled away. "I'll be in the lobby the whole time."

She nodded. "Okay," she said. "Thank you so much."

Ryan kissed her again. "Now go to work."

Janice turned away and walked into the building. We waited for her to disappear in the elevator before we went inside. We sat in a chair behind a pillar and Cortland opened his laptop.

"I have to get onto their server, but I don't have a username. What's your boss's full name?"

"Carl Rogers."

"Okay," he said as he typed quickly. "Are you assigned a

password here?"

"Yes."

"Okay," he said again.

Ryan and I sat beside Cortland while he worked for the next half hour. He insisted that uploading the video as a virus would ensure Carl was dismissed and there were legal consequences if it was broadcast in such a public way. Also, it humiliated him, which was a bonus for me.

"They will realize where the virus came from eventually, but at that point, it won't matter," he said. "We'll be gone." He clicked on a few screens then eventually removed his hand from the keyboard. "It's ready." He smiled. He turned the laptop towards me. "Scarlet, will you do the honors?"

I smiled at him. "I would love to."

"Press enter."

I stared at the button for a moment as I relived the night he attacked me. It was one of the worst nights of my life. Never had I felt so weak and vulnerable. When Carl came at me, I didn't fight until the last moment, and after he chased me from the building, I still didn't seek justice. Since I was such a coward, Carl had taken advantage of Janice, my best friend, and violated her. My hand shook as I reached for the key. I was overwhelmed that this moment of retribution had finally arrived. I felt like I was about to press the button on a bomb, blowing Carl into oblivion. After I took a deep breath, I placed my finger over the button and pressed enter.

The video popped open on the screen and began playing. Cortland closed the laptop and shoved it into his bag. "It will keep playing over and over until someone stops the virus," he said. He stood up and we followed him. "Let's get out of the building."

We walked outside the entryway and stood in front of the doors, waiting for something to happen. I opened my phone and texted Janice, asking her what was going on. She told me that the video was playing on every computer.

I smiled at Cortland. "It worked."

He nodded. "I knew it would."

I text Janice again, but she didn't say anything. I assumed her silence meant she was being questioned by security or human resources. Two cop cars pulled up to the curb outside the entrance, and I felt my heart jump with joy. The police officers walked into building to retrieve Carl. I was practically skipping with happiness. When the cops returned to the lobby with a man handcuffed between them, my heart raced. They opened the doors and Carl noticed me standing off to the side and his eyes widened with recognition. He glared at me for a moment as he was escorted to the car and placed in the backseat. Carl continued to stare at me through the window. I smiled at him, enjoying the sensual taste of retribution. The cars pulled away from the curb and sped down the street. I watched until they were out of my sight.

Janice came out of the building and ran to me, hugging me tightly for a long moment. "Thank you so much," she said. She turned to Cortland and hugged him tightly, making him cough by the force of her constriction. He patted her on the shoulder. "Thank you," she said. Then, she turned to Ryan and kissed him.

"Are you getting just as sick of this as I am?" Cortland asked with a smile.

I watched my brother embrace Janice, and my heart ached. It reminded me of Sean. I felt the tears bubble to the surface as I remembered our amazing relationship. He was the love of my life, but I would never be with him again. I missed him so much and that just made me feel worse. I should be over him. Cortland caught my look and he sighed, feeling bad for inflicting the emotion. He wrapped his arms around me and held me tightly, letting me dissolve inside of his protection.

"It's going to be okay," he whispered.

I pulled away from him and wiped my tears.

Janice was still talking to Ryan. "I'll see you after work," she said.

"My plane leaves at seven," he said. "What time are you off?"

"Five," she said. "I'll try to leave early so I can go with you to the airport."

Ryan nodded. "Okay," he said sadly. "I'll wait at the apartment for you until five thirty, but I have to leave after that."

"I'll try to make it," she said. She kissed him again then waved to us before she went back in the building. My brother watched her go, and I could see the pain in his eyes. I walked over to him and hugged him. Ryan wrapped his arms around me and held me close.

"Why do I always pick the wrong ones?" he asked.

"Why is Janice the wrong one?"

He pulled away. "She says she wants to be with me, but she doesn't believe in long-distance relationships. I can't move here because of you and my shop, and she can't leave for Seattle. It's too soon—we just met."

"I'm sorry, Ryan."

He nodded, but didn't say anything.

"Janice is an editor like you, right?" Cortland asked.

"Yes," I said. I looked at Cortland with a confused expression. Ryan was in pain and Cortland wanted to talk about her profession. I didn't understand the relevance.

"What if you offered her a job at your company?" Cortland asked. "She can edit her own manuscripts and collect the money, which probably pays more than working here anyway, and she'll be getting experience from a successful company, and her best friend will be her boss. It's your company, so it's your decision, but it's just a suggestion."

I looked away from Cortland and to my brother. His face was still set in a frown and I knew he didn't want to put me in that situation. The company was mine exclusively, and I never planned on sharing it with anyone.

"You don't have to, Scar," he said. "I understand."

"Of course, I'll ask her," I said. "I love Janice."

Ryan smiled. "You mean it? You would do that for me?"

"I would do anything for you—you know that."

Ryan picked me up in his arms and spun me around like I was a child. When he dropped me on the ground, he kissed my cheek then picked me up again. I started laughing at his enthusiasm, and Cortland joined me. Ryan finally returned me to the ground.

"Thank you so much," he said. "Thank you."

"You're lucky that I'm not being a brat right now."

Ryan smiled. "You are the best sister in the world."

"Now you're just kissing my ass." I laughed. "I already said yes."

"When are you going to talk to her?"

"Next time I see her."

Ryan nodded. "I hope she says yes."

"I have a feeling she will."

"Let's go out and celebrate," Cortland suggested. "We've put that fucker where he belongs, and now Ryan finally has a girlfriend. Let's eat."

"Where do you want to go?" I asked as we walked down the street.

"I'll eat anything," Ryan said.

"You are such a monkey," I said.

"What's that supposed to mean?" He laughed.

"They eat anything," I said. "Even their own poop."

Ryan shook his head. "I am so happy right now that I don't even care."

Cortland stopped walking when we approached a food cart. "I think I know what Scarlet wants." He smiled.

We were halted in front of a hotdog cart, the very one that I ate at a few weeks earlier. I rolled my eyes. "Here it goes."

"So, do they always drop them on the ground for you, or does that cost extra?" Cortland teased.

"I could kill you," I said.

"Actually, a hotdog sounds pretty good," Ryan said.

"Did you not hear what Cortland just said?" I laughed.

"I'll save some money and ask them not drop mine on the ground," Ryan said sarcastically.

"I can't believe we're doing this," I said as we got in line. We stood there for a moment. Then I heard my name being called. I recognized the voice, but I couldn't put a face to it.

"Scarlet?" Brian said as he came up to me.

I stared at him in surprise. There are seven million people in the city, and I happen to run into Sean's friend. "Hey, Brian," I said. "What are the odds?"

He was holding a bag over his shoulder like he just got off work. "You look great," he said. "What are you doing here?"

I thought for a moment. "I'm visiting."

"Wow," he said. "Sean is lucky to have you. I don't think I would have come back to him—even if Penelope lied to him."

I felt my heart race. "What are you talking about?"

Brian stared at me. "You're here for Sean, right? He hasn't been to work in a week. I'm pretty sure Mr. Perkins fired him. He never answers his phone, so he probably just left a message."

"Why hasn't he been to work?" I asked hysterically. "What's going on?"

"You don't know?" he asked.

"No," I snapped. "Now tell me."

Brian shifted his weight. "I'm sorry. I just assumed that Sean called you," he said. "Well, Penelope lied to him about the baby—the guy she left Sean for is the father. Apparently, when the guy found out she was pregnant, he dumped her. Penelope lost her job because she was so depressed, so she turned to Sean because she had nowhere else to go. After I told Sean everything, he disappeared—I haven't seen him since."

"Did you call him?"

"Yeah," he said. "His phone is off. I even went to the apartment but no one answered."

My emotions were racing. I was furious that Penelope had tricked Sean that way. If he hadn't found out the truth, he would have raised a kid that wasn't even his. Now Sean was missing from work, and even his friend didn't know how he was.

Brian stared at me while I was lost in thought. "So, are you seeing anyone?" he asked with a hopeful voice.

I was so distraught by his news that I didn't even react. Cortland wrapped his arm around my waist and looked at Brian. "Yes, she is," he said. "Now step off."

Brian took a step back. "Well, it was nice seeing you, Scarlet." He turned around and walked up the street, blending in with the mass of people flooding the sidewalk.

My heart was racing so fast in my chest that I thought it would burst. Sean didn't deserve to be treated like that, and it broke my heart knowing he had suffered through it. But then a part of me felt the bitter anger return. He chose her over me even though he knew how she was. The woman cheated on him, had been cheating on him for months before she ended it. I warned Sean that would happen, but he didn't listen to me. He got what he deserved.

When I looked at Ryan, he was already staring at me. "I don't know what to do," I whispered. "Sean chose Penelope of over me—he left me. We were perfect together, but he still wanted to be with her—marry her. He doesn't deserve my compassion or empathy, but I still want to go to him. What do I do?"

Ryan was quiet for a moment. "I can't make that decision for you."

I sighed. "Sean just stopped going to work and no one knows what happened to him. He needs me. I—I can't just go home without checking on him."

Ryan placed his hand on my arm. "I think what Sean did to you was unforgivable, and I don't think he deserves a second chance, but he's still your friend, Scarlet. Even when you hurt each other, all of that becomes irrelevant when you need one other. If you didn't go to him, what kind of friend would you be?"

Even after I ignored Ryan for an entire year, he still took me in when I landed on his doorstep. I didn't even call him to tell him I was coming. What I did was unforgivable and wrong, but Ryan put that aside in light of my pain. When I slept with his friend, he still pardoned it because he knew how upset I was. Without Ryan's help, I really don't know how I would have survived—become the strong person I was.

"I have to go to him."

Ryan nodded. "I know."

15

When I arrived at Sean's door, I took a deep breath before I knocked. If Sean didn't answer, I didn't know what I was going to do. I'd already called him, but it went straight to his voice mail, and the recording said his inbox was full. If he wasn't there, I didn't know where else to look. Now I understood how Sean felt when I left.

I knocked on the door, but there was no answer. I pounded my fist into the wood again, but I heard no sounds from the apartment. Frustrated, I banged my fists against the door for a few seconds before I stopped and stepped back. The sound of moving feet could be distinguished in the apartment. I felt my heart race as I heard the lock unbolt.

When Penelope opened the door, I heard myself gasp in surprise. She was the last person I expected to open the door. After what she did to Sean, I couldn't believe that she was still there.

"Scarlet?" she asked.

The anger coursed through my body as I looked at her. Her stomach bulged out slightly, and I notice it lift up her shirt.

"Is Sean here?" I asked.

She shifted her weight and looked at me apprehensively. "He doesn't want to see anyone."

The door flew open under my force, and Penelope stepped

back.

"Another lie, I presume?" I said as I looked around the apartment. He was nowhere in sight. His bedroom door was closed, and I assumed that he was barricading himself inside of it. I turned back to Penelope and glared at her. "You're lucky that I refuse to hit a pregnant woman."

I walked to the door and tried to open the handle, but it was locked. "Open the door, Sean." There was no sound from inside the room. I knocked on the door again, but there was still no movement. There were paper clips on the kitchen table, so I grabbed one and jammed it inside the lock, picking at it until the handle was free. I pushed the door opened and stopped when I got inside.

There was trash everywhere; cans of beer and glass bottles of hard liquor. The smell of the alcohol was potent and it irritated my nose and made me cough. There were stains in the carpet from the half empty glasses that fell over when Sean stumbled around the room. Prescription bottles were littered around the floor, and I recognized the strong pain killer from the label. When I looked up, Sean was lying on the bed, completely passed out and covered in sweat. I ran my hand over his head and felt the heat from his body. His heartbeat was strong, so I knew he wasn't dying. I shook him and tried to wake him up, but it was useless. He was completely out.

Against my internal objections, I started to cry. The sight of him broken and practically dead made my soul snap in half. Sean didn't deserve that. Even though he betrayed me, he still shouldn't have to go through that. I wished he had called me before it got that bad. My tears stopped falling and I wiped them away.

His room was filthy and dark, so I decided to clean it up. I grabbed a few trash bags and cleared out everything in the room, tossing all the empty glasses and prescription bottles, and then I tore the loose sheets off his bed and put them in the washer. When I vacuumed and dusted his room, Sean still didn't wake up from the sound, and I wondered what combination of drugs and alcohol he took to make him that immobile. Since Sean was still unconscious, I ran to the store and bought groceries, stuffing his refrigerator with healthy food and snacks. I blatantly ignored Penelope while she sat on the couch and avoided my gaze. I wasn't sure why she was still there, but I didn't ask. Sean was killing himself in his own bedroom and Penelope hadn't done a single thing to stop him. The knowledge was enough to make me want to kill her.

When I went back in the bedroom, Sean was still sleeping. I remade his bed while he was still on the mattress, rolling him back and forth while I tucked in the sheet. It wasn't until hours later that Sean opened his eyes. He immediately reached for his nightstand, grabbing for a bottle that was no longer there. When he realized it was gone, he sat up.

Sean was shirtless and I could see the sweat on his chest. I sat at the edge of the bed and didn't move while he fully woke up. I didn't want to frighten him with my sudden appearance, so I waited for him to acknowledge me.

Sean finally looked at me, but he didn't react. He blinked as he stared at me then ran his hands through his hair. I knew he thought he was hallucinating, still high from the prescription drugs.

"I'm real," I whispered.

Sean stared at me. "Scarlet?" he said quietly.

"Yes."

"I know it isn't you," he said. "It's never you."

I got up and moved closer to him. Gently, I placed my hand on his cheek then rubbed him. "I'm here," I said. "It's okay, Sean."

Sean took a deep breath and his chest started to heave in pain. He placed his hand over mine and started to cry. "You came?" he asked.

"Yes," I whispered.

Sean started to sob hysterically while I held him in my arms. I rocked him back and forth for an hour before he was able to calm down. His breathing slowed and his glands ran dry. I kissed his cheeks and whispered comforting words to him as he returned to a state of calm.

"You shouldn't be here," he said. "I don't deserve you."

"I will always care about you, Sean."

"Well, you shouldn't," he said. "You should leave."

"What you did to me broke my heart into a million pieces, Sean, but it doesn't change our friendship. First and foremost, I am your friend—*your best friend*. Everything that has happened is irrelevant at this point. You need help."

Sean nodded. "After I learned the truth I—I just fell. I wanted to die."

"I know."

"The moment I came back, I regretted the decision I made, Scarlet. It was obvious that Penelope didn't love me. She didn't want to be a family anymore. She couldn't care less about the kid. She just needed a place to live and someone to support her. I realized that our relationship had always been that way, but I never noticed it because I was in love with her—but now I'm in love with you."

I didn't know what to say. I anticipated this topic, but I didn't want to discuss it. Sean and I were over—never getting back together. He was so emotional and vulnerable that I didn't want to hurt him, so I said nothing.

"We should get you in the shower—you'll feel better."

"Okay," he whispered. He looked around his bedroom and realized it was empty. All the bottles were gone and the sheets were changed. The curtains that blocked the light in his room were absent, letting the street lights filter into the room. "You cleaned everything."

"Yes," I said. "And after you take a shower, we are going to have dinner."

Sean took a deep breath. "I can't believe you are taking care of me after what I did to you."

I grabbed his hand and squeezed it. "Nothing will change this," I said as I caressed his fingers. "When you can't rely on anything else in the world, know that you always have this."

Sean sighed. "I love you so much," he whispered.

"I love you too," I said. I stood up and walked into the bathroom. "Now let's get you cleaned up." I pulled out a fresh towel from the cabinet and got the water running. When I returned to the bedroom, Sean was still sitting on the bed. "Come on." I smiled.

Sean reached for the wall and got to his feet slowly. His muscles were lean from the weight he lost, and I could see how weak he was. He could barely walk. I wrapped his arm around my shoulder and helped him into the bathroom. Then, I helped him pull off his clothes. Sean didn't seem to be uncomfortable being naked in front of me, and I respected his privacy as much as possible by averting my gaze or keeping my eyes closed.

"I don't care if you look at me," he whispered.

I opened the shower door and got him inside. He couldn't stand so he sat on the shower floor, letting the water wash over him. I watched him for a moment then returned to his bedroom, putting on his old gym clothes before I walked back into the shower. He looked up when I came inside the shower and started washing his body and shampooing his hair. Sean closed his eyes and let me pamper him as the water fell on his body. The sight of him so weak made my heart throb in pain. He was unrecognizable.

After I rinsed out all the foam, I helped him to his feet and turned off the shower. Then I dried him off with a towel. When he wasn't dripping with water, we walked back into the bedroom and

I helped him into his running shorts and a shirt. I dried myself off and put on the outfit that I had been wearing earlier.

Sean lay on top of the bed with his eyes open, saying nothing as he stared at the ceiling. I sat next to him and ran my fingers through his damp hair.

"I'm going to make dinner," I said as I got up.

Sean looked at me. "You're going to cook for me?" he asked sadly.

"Yes," I said as I ran my hands down his arms. "You need some food. Are you hungry?"

He nodded. "What are you making?"

"I was going to make chicken marsala."

"That sounds good," he whispered.

"I'll be back in a little while."

"Okay," he said. "I'm tired." He closed his eyes and I pulled the sheet over him, tucking him in like a child. When I left his bedroom, I started crying again, overwhelmed by his broken frame. I started cooking in the kitchen and ignored Penelope as she watched television on the couch. When everything was ready, I put the food on two plates and poured two glasses of water, ready to bring him into Sean's room. The sight of Penelope sitting on Sean's couch made me so angry that I placed the plates on table and walked over to her.

"Why the fuck are you still here?"

The venom in my voice made her jump. "Sean said I could stay here."

"Why?" I asked. "He doesn't owe you anything. Get the hell out of his life, Penelope—for good."

"I have nowhere else to go," she whispered.

"So, you used Sean because you can't take care of yourself?"

She looked away from me and didn't say anything.

I was so livid that I started laughing, almost hysterically, and she moved away from me on the couch, frightened by my maniacal behavior. "You know what's funny?" I asked. "If you had just told Sean the truth, he would have taken you in and supported you. Hell—he probably would have helped you raise the kid because he's so in love with you. You are so stupid, Penelope. You have no idea what you threw away." The sight of her saddened expression was enough for me to end the verbal attack. The gleam of a diamond on her ring caught my eye, and when I looked down at her hand, I saw the engagement ring that Sean got for her. He'd finally proposed to her. The pain and betrayal washed over me, but I pushed it back, knowing it was irrelevant at that point. I turned away and grabbed the plates then walked into Sean's room. I returned for the water and slammed the door behind me.

I helped Sean sit up in bed then I placed the food on his lap. He looked at his plate and picked up his fork, barely able to hold it in his hand. The sight made me want to cry. I could kill Penelope. Sean ate very slowly, chewing his food longer than normal, and he took a long time just to bring the fork to his mouth. I sat across from him while I ate my dinner. We didn't speak until Sean put aside his plate and drank the entire glass of water.

He looked at me. "Thank you," he said. "I can't remember the last time I ate real food."

I nodded, too emotional to speak. I grabbed his plate and placed them in the kitchen sink, then returned with a new glass of water. Sean quickly emptied the glass.

"Would you like more?" I asked.

"No," he whispered as he sat back against his pillows. "Thank you, Scarlet."

I grabbed his hand and held it. "You don't need to thank me. You would have done it for me."

"But that's different," he whispered. "You actually deserve it."

I didn't know what to say. I looked away.

"How long are you staying?" he asked.

"As long as it takes for you to get better," I said.

He nodded. "I don't think I'll ever be better, Scar."

"You'll get there."

"Not without you," he whispered.

I got up from the bed and searched in his drawer, looking for clean clothes to wear. I knew where this conversation was going and I wanted to avoid it. I grabbed some shorts and a shirt and walked into the bathroom to change. When I returned to the bedroom, I pulled back the blankets and crawled inside, lying next to him. Sean watched me for a moment then started to get up.

"What are you doing?" I asked.

"I'll sleep on the floor," he said. "You don't have to sleep with me."

I grabbed his shoulder and pulled him back. "Please don't do that," I said. "Stay here with me."

"I don't deserve to sleep beside you."

Since Sean was so weak, I was able to pull him back to bed and under the covers. "I want to sleep with you."

Sean sighed. "Okay. I won't do anything."

"I know," I said as I wrapped my arm around his waist. Sean turned on his side then pulled me to his chest, resting his face in the crook of my neck. He sighed deeply as he held me, and I could feel his heart thudding in his chest at a fast pace.

"Thank you for coming to me," he whispered in my ear. "You have no idea how much it means to me. I thought you hated me."

"I never could," I said.

"You are amazing." Sean didn't move away as he held me tightly. I could tell he wasn't going to let go.

"Why is Penelope still here?"

Sean didn't answer for a moment. "She has no one else."

"That isn't your problem."

"And I'm not your problem either."

I sighed. In the end, it was love that controlled your decisions, not hate. If that weren't the case, Ryan would have kicked me out when I arrived on his doorstep. I never would have given Sean another chance, and Penelope would be homeless.

"I love you," I said.

Sean took a deep breath. "I love you, Scar."

His breathing became deep and shallow, and I knew he was falling asleep. I ran my hands through his hair while he held me close to him. I could feel him relaxing the longer we stayed still. My phone rang from my nightstand, and I reached for it while Sean still held onto me.

"Hello?" I said when I answered it.

"It's Ryan."

"Hey," I said quietly.

"How is everything? Is Sean okay?"

I was quiet for a moment. "No, he isn't, but we're working on it."

"I think you did the right thing."

"I do too."

"My flight is leaving soon," he said. "Janice is changing in her room. I was hoping you could talk to her before I left. I realize that you're busy with Sean, but could you talk to her before I head out?"

"Of course," I said. "Put her on the phone."

Sean still clutched me tightly, refusing to let me go. His face was still buried in my neck and his heart started to race again.

"Hello?" she said with a smile in her voice.

"Hey," I said. "Can you move away from Ryan for a minute?"

"Sure," she said. "Hold on." I heard a door close. "I'm in my room."

"How much do you like my brother?" I asked. "And be honest with me. If you tell me you aren't that interested, that's fine. It won't change our friendship."

"Of course, I like him," she said. "I thought that was obvious."

"If I could get you a job in Seattle working in publishing, making the salary you make now, would you move there for him?"

Janice was quiet for a moment. "We just met, Scarlet."

"So, that's a no."

She sighed. "That's just a huge lifestyle change for a guy I just met," she said. "I like Ryan a lot. I hate to see him go, but I can't sacrifice everything for him."

"Okay," I said. "That's reasonable. So you are just going to breakup then?"

Janice was quiet for a moment. "I—I don't know. I guess we could do long-distance."

"But you don't believe long-distance relationships work."

"Then I don't know what to do, Scar—I really like him."

"If you can see yourself loving him, then I think you should do it. You've been single forever because every guy you date is a loser. Ryan is the first guy you've dated that you actually like. I know that Ryan is falling hard for you and he never feels this way."

"Would he want me to move to Seattle? I mean, wouldn't

that scare him off?"

"He's the reason we are having this conversation." I laughed. "I wouldn't be surprised if he's already in love with you."

Janice was quiet.

"So, if you had a job in Seattle, would you move for him?"

"You can't guarantee that."

"Hypothetically, would you do it? If you had a place to stay with Ryan and I, and you had job security, would you do it?"

Janice was quiet for a moment, thinking to herself. She said nothing for a while and I could hear her bite her nails over the phone. "Yes."

I smiled. "You mean that?"

"I know this is crazy, but yes, I would. Besides, there is nothing for me in the city. My best friend lives in Seattle."

"So, you are willing to do this?"

"I sound like a crazy person." She laughed.

"I have to tell you something, Janice. Now that you have agreed to move to Seattle, I would like to offer you a job. I own my own editing company and it's been doing really well. You can edit your manuscript on your own time and it pays good money. The position is yours if you want it."

Janice screamed. "Why didn't you tell me?"

"I wanted to make sure you were moving for Ryan—not because of the job."

"This is amazing, Scarlet. I hate working for someone else."

"Well, technically you are working for me."

"You know what I mean."

"You are officially hired, Janice."

She screamed again. "I'll put in my two weeks tomorrow and start packing right away."

"You know what you should do first?"

"What?" she asked.

"Tell Ryan."

I could hear the smile in her voice. "He's going to be so happy."

"I know."

I heard her bedroom door open as she walked into the other room. She handed the phone to Ryan.

"Hey," he said. "How'd it go?"

"I'll let Janice tell you," I said. "I just wanted to let you know I'm not flying home with you. I'm staying in New York until Sean is back on his feet. His laptop is here so I can keep working—don't worry about the money."

"Let me know when you're coming home."

"I will."

"And Scarlet?" he said.

"What?"

"I love you." The sound of happiness in his voice was evident. I imagined Janice standing in front of him, smiling at him while he talked on the phone. The look was all he needed. He knew Janice was moving.

"I love you, too."

I hung up the phone and put it on the nightstand. Sean released his hold on me long enough for me to roll over and come back.

"What was that about?" he asked.

"Well, a lot of things have happened."

"Tell me."

"Ryan, Cortland, Janice, and I caught my boss sexually harassing Janice on tape, and we released it on the server at work. Janice and Ryan are together now and she is moving to Seattle to be with him."

Sean stared at me, taking in all the information slowly. "That's great," he said. "I'm happy for Ryan."

"Janice told me what you did, Sean."

He dropped his gaze and avoided my look.

"I'm not mad at you."

He sighed. "I thought you would be furious with me."

"I just can't believe you did that."

"I would do anything for you, Scarlet. Just knowing that guy touched you made me snap. I can't even remember beating him. All I recall is the rage that was coursing through me."

"He was in a coma for three days."

"Good," he whispered. "And I'm glad that you brought him down Scarlet—I'm proud of you."

"I am too."

"If that guy ever comes near you, I'll kill him."

"Since I'll be living in Seattle, I don't think that's likely."

Sean nodded, but didn't say anything. He returned his face to my neck and closed his eyes, sighing deeply. "Will you be here when I wake up?"

"I might be cooking breakfast."

"Please don't," he said. "I need to see you when I wake up. That's always the hardest part."

I felt the tears fall from my eyes at his words. Knowing he was in so much pain killed me. I would take it all away if I could. "Okay." I closed my eyes and fell asleep in Sean's arms, feeling his heart slow in his chest until he finally fell asleep.

16

When I woke up the next morning, I didn't move. Sean said he wanted to see me when he woke up, so I didn't leave the bed. Patiently, I waited for him to wake up and see me lying in his arms, exactly where he left me the night before.

Finally, Sean opened his eyes and looked at me. He sighed deeply when he met my gaze then he pulled me closer to him. "I'm so glad that you're here."

"Me too," I said.

Sean had beads of sweat on his forehead and he felt warm. He had been sweating all night. It must be a side effect from all the booze he drank and the pills he swallowed. When Sean was indisposed, I threw everything away, making sure he wouldn't do that to himself again.

"Do you have a special request for breakfast?" I smiled.

"I'll eat anything," he said.

I got up from the bed and walked over to his side. "Get ready while I make breakfast."

"For what?" he asked.

"For basic hygiene purposes." I laughed.

"I've been really disgusting this past week." He smiled.

"I know," I said. "I cleaned your room."

"I'm so embarrassed." He sighed.

"It's okay," I said. "I ate a hotdog off the ground."

Sean started laughing and I loved the sound. I hoped that he was starting to feel better. He had improved dramatically in just one day. A good night's rest and a healthy meal had helped him immensely. Sean moved to the edge of the bed and placed both feet on the floor. He helped himself get up and he stood still for a moment, keeping his balance before he took a step forward. I held his arm as he walked into the bathroom. He made it to the sink without much assistance.

"I think I'm okay," he said as he leaned over the sink.

I rubbed his back as he looked at himself in the mirror. "Are you sure?"

He nodded.

"I'm going to cook breakfast," I said. "Let me know if you need anything."

"I will." I shut the bathroom door behind me and started cooking in the kitchen. Penelope was sleeping on the couch, but I made no effort to be quiet while I turned on the water or cooked over the stove. I placed the pancakes, bacon, and eggs on the plate and carried a glass of orange juice into the bedroom. I left and returned with my own plate and placed it on the bed. Sean was still in the bathroom with the door closed.

"Are you okay?" I asked as I knocked lightly.

"Yes," he said quietly. I heard him gag and knew he was vomiting. When I opened the door, he was leaning over the toilet seat with his head in his hands, breathing deeply with his eyes closed. I kneeled behind him and rubbed his back while he finished emptying his stomach. Finally, he stopped and flushed the bowl. Sean wiped his face with the towel that I held in my hands, and I helped him to his feet. He washed his face and rinsed out his mouth with mouthwash.

"Do you feel better?" I asked as I rubbed his back.

"Yes," he said with nod. "I always feel better after I throw up."

Sean dried his face and walked back into the bedroom. He didn't need my help as he sat on the bed and leaned against the headboard. He stared at the food on the plates.

"It's okay if you aren't hungry," I said.

Sean pulled the plate to him. "I'm starving," he said. "Thank you."

He started shoveling the food into his mouth. I was surprised that he had an appetite until I realized that he probably threw up often because of the alcohol in his system. Hopefully, that was the last time he would need to vomit. Sean finished his plate and drank his glass of juice.

"Thank you for cooking for me," he said.

I nodded as I took our plates to the sink in the kitchen. When I came back into the room, Sean was still sitting on the bed.

"Let's go to the park," I said. "I think you need to get out of this apartment."

"I don't think I can handle a lot of walking or running."

"We can just sit on a blanket in the shade," I said. "But if you're too weak, that's fine."

Sean was quiet for a moment. "I can handle that."

"Okay," I said as I grabbed an extra blanket from the cabinet and placed it on the bed. Sean changed into jeans and a shirt while I wore the outfit I had on the day before. We slowly made our way to the park down the street and eventually found a vacant spot in the shade of a tree. Sean and I sat down after I laid out the blanket on the grass. There was a father and son playing baseball a few feet away, and we watched them for a while. Sean was very quiet, and I was afraid that he wasn't feeling well.

"Are you doing okay?" I asked.

"Yes," he said. "I'm just not used to being outside."

Sean moved closer to me and held my hand in his. I felt him caress my fingers with his own while we stared at the joggers who ran down the path with their dogs on leashes. We said nothing for a long time.

"When are you leaving?" he asked.

"When I think you're ready."

"Well, you should set a time frame because I'm never going to be ready for you to leave, Scar." He didn't drop my hand while he sat under the shade of the tree.

"You're going to be okay."

Sean shook his head and said nothing.

"Why did you do it, Sean?"

He understood my meaning. "I didn't care anymore. I lost

everything and I had nothing to live for. It made no difference if I lived or died."

"Just because Penelope betrayed you?" I asked. "Penelope already hurt you once. How could she do it again?"

"It wasn't because of Penelope." He sighed. "It's because of you. You are the greatest thing that ever happened to me and I messed it up. I made a mistake. Without you, I have no purpose— no reason to go on."

"Please don't say that."

"Okay," he said. Sean dropped the conversation and said nothing for a few moments. He finally looked at me. "I'm not saying this because I'm trying to win you over—I know you will never take me back—but so you know the truth. As soon as I got back to the city, I regretted the choice I made. I thought I made the right decision for my child—having a complete family. With you, I was happy and complete—with her, I was empty. I realized that you are the love of my life, Scar. I thought it was her, but I was wrong—it's you."

"You were never over her," I said.

Sean sighed. "No, I wasn't," he said. "But that doesn't mean I didn't want to be. I can honestly say I have no such feelings anymore."

"You chose her over me, Sean—that's what it comes down to. Instead of being a father in the kid's life, you chose to be her husband and a father. You never had to be. That was something you wanted for yourself."

"You really don't understand where I am coming from?" he asked incredulously. "That my actions were for my kid only? It had nothing to do with Penelope. I didn't even want her, Scar."

"Yes," I said. "But it doesn't change or justify what you did. I even told you I had no problem with being a stepmother—I would love your kid like it was my own. You still chose her, Sean." I felt the tears bubble under my eyes and stream down my face. Sean released my hand and wrapped his arms around me, letting me cry into his shoulder. "I can forgive you for what you did, but I'll never forgive you for throwing us away. I've never been happier in my whole life than when I was with you, Sean— never."

Sean started to cry and I felt his tears drip down my neck. "I know," he whispered. "I made the biggest mistake of my life."

I pulled away from him and wiped my tears away. "I don't want to talk about this ever again."

Sean sighed. "Does this mean I never have a chance with you?" he asked. "We could start over and take it slow. I know you understand how much I love you, Scarlet. It was obvious every moment we were together."

"But not when we were apart," I said. "You cheated on me."

Sean stared at me. "I never did anything with Penelope before I ended things with you," he said. "I've never lied to you and I'm not now."

"No," I said.

"What does that mean?"

"We are over Sean—done."

"We can take a break and start over when this is settled," he said. "We are meant for each other. Please give me another chance."

"It's over."

Sean dropped his gaze. "Scarlet—"

"My answer will not change. I deserve to be with someone who doesn't have to fuck up twice to realize how amazing I am."

"I agree," he said. "But luckily for me, I am the only guy you want."

"For now," I said.

Sean looked at me. "This can't be the end."

"But it is."

17

Sean didn't mention our relationship for the next two days. I was thankful for the reprieve because I was emotionally dry from thinking about it. He improved over the following days. He wasn't vomiting his food anymore, and he didn't wake up every morning covered in a cold sweat. My time with Sean was coming to an end. At night, I indulged myself by wrapping my arms around him while I slept until the morning light broke through the windows and flooded his room. I even stared at him while he slept, treasuring the memory for safekeeping through the following years. I suspected that was the last time I would see Sean, at least for many years, and even that seemed unlikely. My whole family lived in Seattle now. There was nothing left for me in New York.

When Sean woke up, I walked into the living room and searched through Penelope's clothes until I found a black dress and shoes that I let her borrow months ago.

"I'm taking these back," I said without looking at her.

Sean watched me walk into the bathroom then stared at me when I came out. "Are you leaving?" he asked sadly.

"Yes," I said. "But I'll be back. I have to run an errand."

"I'll come with you," he said as got up.

"I'm going alone, Sean."

He stared at me. "Why are you dressed like that?"

"I just want to look nice."

"Are you going on a date?" he asked apprehensively.

"No."

"Then why won't you tell me where you're going?"

I sighed. "Please drop it, Sean."

He was quiet for a moment. "Okay."

"There is breakfast on the stove," I said. "I'll be back in an hour." The cab took me downtown to the building that housed Sean's firm.

When I walked through the hallway of the office, Brian spilled his coffee on his shirt as he watched me pass him. He didn't say anything as he stared at me. He was speechless. Mr. Perkins' name was on the outside of the door, so I knew which office was his. I knocked on the door and I heard him speak.

"Come in."

When I walked into the room, his eyes widened in surprise then his mouth stretched into a smile. It was obvious that he approved of my tight fitted dress and the way my hair fell around my shoulders. I reached out and shook his hand. "It's nice to see you again, sir."

"The pleasure is all mine," he said happily as he held my hand. He didn't release his hold and I didn't fight it. "What can I do for you?"

"I was hoping I could speak with you."

"Well, you have my undivided attention," he said as he glanced to my legs and back up to my face. My tolerance for men was waning, but I forced myself to focus on my mission.

"I wanted to discuss Sean."

Mr. Perkins nodded. "You are referring to the man that just stopped showing up for work without calling or giving notice? This is the Sean you are referring to?"

"Yes," I said with nod. "The very one."

"I sincerely hope he doesn't expect to get his job back," he said. "I've already hired a replacement."

"I understand that," I said. "What Sean did was inexcusable and unprofessional. You won't hear me say otherwise."

"You aren't making a compelling argument." He laughed.

"It was never my intention to."

"Then what do you want?" he asked. He leaned against his desk while he looked at me, mesmerized by my appearance. At least I could rely on my looks when I had nothing else to offer.

"I want you to give Sean a second chance."

"I have no reason to," he said.

"I am sure that you know what happened to him, sir. I know it's been the office gossip around here."

"I'm not saying I don't feel bad for the guy."

"Sean was a great worker and employee. He never called in sick and he never caused any trouble. If you have any compassion or empathy for him, please give him another chance, sir."

Mr. Perkins stared at me for a moment. "What did he do to get the love of such an amazing woman?" he asked. "You could have anyone you want. Why that guy?"

I sighed. "Sean is also amazing," I said. "That may not always be clear, but it's true. I'll stand by him forever."

"I can't think of very many women who would do what you are doing right now," he said. "He's a lucky man."

"I know," I said. "And he knows that, too."

"Tell him I'll see him tomorrow," he said as he walked back to his seat. I felt my face stretch into a smile. "And if he messes up one time, he's done. Even if he is a minute late, he's fired."

I walked over to him and shook his hand vigorously. Then, I kissed him on the cheek and pulled away. "Thank you so much, Mr. Perkins."

His smile was wider than I had ever seen it. "You are very welcome, Scarlet."

I left his office and walked past Brian's desk. He was trying to get the coffee stain out of his shirt, so he didn't see me make my departure. I called down a cab and returned to Sean's apartment. When I walked in his bedroom, he was sitting up in bed reading a book. He put it aside when I came inside.

"That was quick," he said.

"It didn't take as long as I planned," I said. "Did you like your breakfast?"

Sean nodded. "Everything you cook is amazing, Scarlet."

"Thank you."

"Now are you going to tell me what you were doing?"

I smiled. "Mr. Perkins gave you your job back," I said

excitedly. "You start tomorrow."

Sean stared at me for a moment, processing what I said. "How did that happen?"

"I talked to your boss."

"And he just hired me back?" he asked incredulously. "I haven't called or emailed the office in a week, and now it's water under the bridge?"

"Well, he said you can't mess around anymore," I said. "Even if you are a minute late, you're done."

"What the hell did you say to him?" he asked.

"I just asked for your job back."

Sean shook his head. "I can't believe you did that for me."

"I can." I smiled. "I would do anything for you."

Sean rose from the bed and hugged me tightly. "Thank you," he whispered. "I don't know what I would do without you."

"Make sure you don't screw it up this time," I teased him. "Otherwise I'm going to have to bring your boss donuts."

Sean smiled at me. "What's better than that? A gorgeous woman holding a box of glazed donuts—every man's fantasy."

"Well, I am a hot piece of ass."

Sean's face fell, and I saw him take a deep breath. The words wounded him and made him step back. The last time I said that, he said I was *his* hot piece of ass. I was no longer his and never would be again. I saw how much I hurt him, and I regretted my words.

"I'm sorry," I whispered.

168

Sean turned around, blocking his face from view, and said nothing for a few moments. When he found his bearings, he turned back to me. "When are you leaving?"

"My flight leaves tomorrow."

Sean nodded. "Okay."

"You are going to be okay."

"How is this going to be?" he asked. "Am I allowed to call you? Can I still come visit you? Will you ever come back to New York?" The pain in his eyes went straight to my heart. I knew he'd been thinking about this for the past few days. It was obvious that he already knew the answer to his question by the tightness of his jaw and the tension in his shoulders.

"No," I said. "We aren't doing any of that."

"Please don't do this to me," he whispered. "Don't cut me out—*please*."

I dropped my gaze. "I can't talk to you or see you anymore, Sean. It's too hard for me. I want to move on, and I can't do that if I'm still in love with you."

"Give me another chance, Scarlet—please. I promise I won't hurt you again."

I shook my head. "Please stop asking me."

Sean crossed his arms over his chest. "At least give me your friendship."

"Sean, if you ever need me for anything, I am here for you—always—no matter what happens. But I can't talk to you on a regular basis. Please respect that. Don't call me unless you absolutely need to. I am moving on with my life—I suggest you do the same."

Sean walked into the bathroom and shut the door behind him. I heard the water running in the shower and knew he was sitting under it, trying to drown out all other noise, including the voices in his head. I changed into his gym clothes and walked into the bathroom. Sean had his head between his legs and I knew he was crying by the shaking of his body. He just had on his undershorts and his clothes were scattered across the floor. I got into the shower and sat next to him. He stopped crying when he realized I was sitting next to him, and I wrapped my arms around him.

"You have to promise me, Sean," I said. "I trust you not to lie to me."

Sean didn't respond. He knew I was asking him to not fall back into the same depression. That he wouldn't turn to substance abuse just to cope. He would stay strong and move on with this life.

"Sean," I pressed. "Promise me."

He sighed. "Okay. I promise."

18

Sean and I left the apartment the next morning with my bag over my shoulder, but Sean carried it for me as we walked down to the sidewalk. Cars and taxis were speeding down the road as people hurried to work in the city. Sean and I stood there for a moment as the noise of the cars and people echoed around us.

Sean stared at me for a long moment, and his look was so sad that I turned around to wave down a cab just to avoid seeing him. Suddenly, Sean broke down and the tears fell from his eyes. The cab pulled over and I opened the door.

"I can't believe this is happening," he said. He grabbed me in his arms and held me close. "Please don't do this to me. I can't live without you, Scar. Don't go."

I pulled away from him. "Yes, you can," I said. "You chose to live without me when you went back to Penelope. If you can do it then, you can do it now. You'll be fine, Sean. You can have whatever girl you want. She'll fall in love with you and you'll be happy again. You'll forget about me in no time. You probably won't even remember my name." It wasn't my intention to be cruel or bitter, but it was the truth. He would be fine without me.

"Please don't say that," he whispered. "I love you."

The tears fell from my eyes as I listened to him. He was heartbroken and scared, and I could hear the sincerity in his voice.

A part of me worried about what he would do after I left, but he promised me that he wouldn't lose control. "I love you, too."

Sean held me for a moment and I felt his tears drip onto my neck. My body shook with my own sobs as I held him for the last time. I didn't expect to see him ever again. This was just as hard for me as it was for him.

"I'll do anything," he said. "Anything to make you stay."

"There is nothing," I whispered. I pulled away and looked at him. "Take care of yourself."

Sean's eyes were red from the tears he shed. His hands gripped my arms so tightly I doubted he would let me go. He pressed his face against mine then I felt his lips on my own. He kissed me gently, and I returned his affection, also depressed that I was saying goodbye. His tears combined with mine and I felt them drip down my face as we kissed on the sidewalk of Manhattan, oblivious to the people walking by and the horn of the cab that was waiting for me. I grabbed his face as I kissed him, and Sean dropped my bag as he held me closer. His lips tasted like salt from his falling tears and it made me cry harder. Finally, I pulled away and grabbed my bag without looking at him. It was already hard enough, without him making it unbearable. I turned to the cab, but Sean grabbed me.

"I'll always love you, Scarlet," he said. "I'm always here if you change your mind."

I still didn't look at him. "I'll always love you, too," I said. "But I'm not coming back."

Sean released his grip on my arm and I sat inside the cab, shutting the door behind me.

"JFK," I said through my tears. The cab sped away and I didn't turn around to look at Sean standing on the sidewalk, watching me disappear from his life forever. I didn't have to see him to know how much pain he was in. He was standing on the corner, crying in front of the entire city, and he didn't care at all. I wanted to be with Sean forever, but I couldn't forgive him for what he did. It was time to move on.

When I was finally on the plane, I called Ryan and told him I was coming home. He seemed excited by the news, and I knew he was happy that he and Janice had worked things out. I was happy for my brother. Ryan deserved to have someone that made him smile.

I looked out the window as the plane took off and could see the buildings of Manhattan in the distance. Hopefully, Sean made it to work on time. Otherwise, he wouldn't have a job. I was glad that Sean was back on his feet. My tears stopped falling when the city was absent from view, and I knew the hardest part was over. I decided to never think about Sean again. While it was a cold attitude, I knew there was no other way for me to get through the pain. Sean and I were over forever—I had to move on.

Cortland was waiting at the gate when I arrived, and I ran into his arms as soon as I saw him. He held me for a moment before he pulled away. "Are you alright?" he asked. I nodded, but didn't say anything. Cortland grabbed my bag from the floor and placed it over his shoulder. We walked to his car in the parking lot, and he helped me get inside. "I'm glad you are home," he said. "I was tired of drinking mega-shakes by myself."

"You went without me?" I smiled.

"I'm sorry," he said. "I just couldn't wait." He reached over and held my hand while he drove back to the apartment Ryan and I shared. "Perhaps you should get it out now while we are alone. I'm assuming you are going to act like everything is okay even though you are absolutely miserable."

"There is nothing to say, really," I whispered. "Nothing has changed."

"So, Sean is history?" he asked. "It's over—he's done."

I nodded. "I'm moving on."

Cortland sighed. "I'm here for you."

"I know."

"So, I guess I should warn you before you get home."

"What do you mean?"

"Well, Janice already moved here," he said. "And her crap is taking up the whole apartment. I'm even storing some of her stuff at my place. That girl has a lot of shit."

I laughed. "That's fine," I said. "I'm happy that she's there."

"You don't think it's too soon?"

"Yes, it is too soon, but I think it works for them. Ryan has never been traditional, and I've never seen Janice so strung on someone. I think the risk is worth it."

174

Cortland pulled up to the sidewalk and we got out of the car. Cortland carried my bag up the stairs and to the apartment. I inserted my key in the lock but Ryan opened the door before I could I turn the handle. He stared at me for a moment, gazing at my saddened features and empty eyes, then he hugged me, holding me for a long time.

"Are you okay?" he whispered.

I forced myself to smile at him. "I'll be fine," I said as I pulled away. Cortland and I walked into the apartment and Janice screamed when she saw me. She wrapped me in her embrace and hugged me tightly.

"I'm so glad you are back."

"Me too." I smiled.

"Is it okay if I live with you?" she asked hesitantly. "Ryan said you wouldn't mind."

"And he's right," I assured her. "We both want you here."

Janice smiled at me. "Are you okay?"

"I'm fine," I said quickly. "Please don't worry about me."

"So, what was wrong with Sean?" Ryan asked. "You were with him for five days."

I sighed. "He just—lost his way."

"What does that mean?" Cortland asked.

"He started abusing prescription drugs and alcohol, and stopped showing up to work. He was so passed out when I got there that I couldn't wake him up. Sean was—low."

Ryan nodded. "How is he now?"

"Good," I said. "He's back to work and back on his feet."

"It's a good thing you were there for him," Ryan said.

"I know."

I looked around the apartment and saw all the boxes of Janice's belongings. "What happened to your two weeks' notice?"

Janice laughed. "R and R is under investigation, so I just decided to leave. Besides, I hated being away from Ryan. He practically forced me to come."

"I can believe that." I smiled.

Cortland walked down the hallway and placed my bag in my room. "I should get going," he said. He turned to me. "Let me know if you need anything, Scar. If these two annoy you too much, my apartment is always open to you—even if you just want to watch television."

I hugged him. "Thanks."

Cortland left and I went into the kitchen to find something to eat. I made a sandwich from the deli meat in the refrigerator then ate it at the table. My body was exhausted but I didn't feel tired. All I felt was depression. Janice came into the living room wearing one of Ryan's shirts and shorts, lounging around the house. She sat on the couch and patted the seat next to her. I walked in and sat beside her.

"What happened?" she asked.

I shrugged my shoulders. "I helped Sean get back on his feet," I said. "That's about it."

"I can't believe he did all that—he must have hit rock

bottom."

"Yes, I think he did."

"Are you going to try to work it out with him?"

"No," I said quickly.

Janice sighed. "I think you did the right thing by going back to him, Scarlet. Imagine what would have happened if you just abandoned him. He might even be dead at this point."

I shook my head. "Please don't say that."

"I know that I have no right to interfere with you and Sean, but I think you should give him another chance."

"You've got to be kidding me."

"No," Janice said quietly. "What he did to you was wrong, but he thought he was making the right decision for his child. He wouldn't have left you if Penelope wasn't pregnant—that was the only reason he went to her."

"Sean said the same thing, but I guess we'll never know."

"Ryan believes him."

"Ryan doesn't know what he's saying."

"Scarlet, Ryan told me how happy you were with him. Just think about giving it another chance. Sean was never this depressed when Penelope left him—he only feels this way because he lost you. It's obvious that he loves you in a way that he never loved Penelope."

"Please drop it, Janice."

"I can't," she said. "I don't want you to regret this."

"I'm tired of being second best. I want to be with someone

that won't screw me over all the time."

Janice sighed. "This was just bad timing. Sean was in a breakup when you slept together. Then, you jumped into a relationship with him right after that. Sean wanted to take it slow, but you were the one who rushed him into it. I know if you gave him a real chance, he would treat you the way you deserve."

"Now I'm starting to hate the fact that you're dating my brother," I snapped. "He can't keep his mouth closed."

"Sean treated Penelope like a goddess," she said. "He isn't a cheat and he isn't a liar—he can give you what you want. Just give him one more chance—just one, Scarlet."

Ryan's footsteps echoed down the hallway, and he looked at us when he came around the corner. "Coming, babe?" he asked her.

"I'll be there in a minute." She smiled.

I jumped from my seat. "We are done here," I said as I walked away. I went into my bedroom and locked the door behind me, falling on my bed like I was paralyzed. Everyone wanted to discuss Sean and that was the last thing I wanted—I just wanted to forget about him.

19

"What is the big deal about this place?" she asked when we took our seats at Mega-Shake. The restaurant was quiet with hushed voices from the few people who were in the joint. Ryan brought our milkshakes from the counter and passed them around. He wrapped his arm around Janice and kissed her cheek before he started to drink his milkshake. The sight made me want to gag.

"Try the shake and you'll see what I mean," I said.

Cortland drank half of his in one gulp. He sat beside me and I could feel his elbow touching my arm, constantly reminding me that he was always there.

Janice took a sip then tasted it for a moment. "Well, it's pretty good."

"*Pretty good*?" Ryan said sarcastically. "Try best thing in the entire world."

"I thought I was?" Janice smiled.

Ryan thought for a moment. "Okay, the second best thing in the world."

"That sounds better," Janice said.

I was happy for my brother, but at the same time, it was hard to see them together. Everything reminded me of Sean, and it made my head want to explode. Ryan caught my saddened expression.

"How are you doing?" he asked with a sad voice.

Every time people asked me that, it made me angry. I saw the pity in their eyes and heard the sadness in their voice and it just irritated me. I was never going to get better unless people started treating me like I was better. "Stop asking me that—you're annoying me."

"Well, how are you?" Ryan asked.

"I'm fine—drop it."

"Have you talked to him?" my brother asked.

"Stop talking about him," I snapped. "Don't mention him anymore."

"So no," he said sarcastically. "You aren't okay."

"Fuck you, Ryan."

Ryan dropped his arm from around Janice's shoulder and leaned closer to me. "Scarlet, I'm just worried about you—that's all."

"Well, don't be."

He stared at me for a moment then ran his hands through his hair. I could tell he was thinking about something. "I think you should try to work this out with Sean."

"You are on team Sean, too?"

"Is there another team to root for?" he asked sarcastically. "I think this whole fiasco was just bad timing. Sean was wrong and I agree with that, but I also think that he's a good guy and deserves another chance. If I didn't know how in love with him you were, I probably wouldn't say anything, but I know that you want him.

Just give him one more chance, Scarlet."

"So much for being a protective brother," I snapped.

"I *am* protecting you," he said. "Just think about it, Scar. Sean went all the way to your office and beat the shit out of your boss. Maybe it hasn't always been clear that he loves you with the Penelope issue, but I know he does. Give it another chance—a real one. And *not* when he just got out of a relationship, *not* when he's living across the country, and *not* when some woman is having his child—but a *real* chance. You have been through so much together and now you are finally on the other side—just be happy."

"This conversation is over," I said. "Please don't bring it up again."

Ryan stared at me then leaned back in his chair. It was awkward for a moment, and none of us said anything for a long time. Janice looked down at her hands and Cortland scratched the Styrofoam on his cup. Ryan looked out the window and avoided my gaze. Janice rose from her seat.

"I'm going to the restroom," she said as she walked away.

When she was out of earshot, Cortland leaned forward. "How is it going with her?" he asked.

"It's great." Ryan smiled. "I've never been happier."

"It doesn't bother you that she's living with you already?"

"No," he said. "I was worried that it might be weird, but I love having her around. I think this is the real thing—at least I hope it is."

"How's the sex?"

"Really good." Ryan smiled.

I rolled my eyes. "Just because I'm close to you doesn't mean you have to go into the details."

Ryan ignored me. "She gives good head."

"Don't be gross," I snapped.

Cortland nodded. "Monnique does too, which is a relief. I could never get Elizabeth to do anything unconventional."

Ryan nodded. "Well, I don't have that problem with her." He smiled.

Janice came back from the bathroom and returned to her seat. "What were you talking about?"

"Ryan says you give good head," I said.

Janice smiled at Ryan. "Well, that was kinda personal."

"It's a compliment." He shrugged. He wasn't embarrassed at all.

She rolled her eyes and looked away.

"I hope you're comfortable with everyone knowing everything about your relationship," I warned. "Because Ryan likes to blab about it."

"As long as it stays within the four us, I don't care."

My cup was only half empty, but I didn't want it anymore. My appetite suddenly vanished. Cortland and Ryan were both finished with theirs, and I could tell Janice was done drinking her shake because she pushed it away from her. Ryan pressured her to eat more, but Janice never had an appetite. She would eat a few bites here and there but she wasn't back to her normal weight.

Moving from New York and quitting her job were factors that continued to stress her out, but I hoped she would return to normal in a few weeks.

"Are you guys ready?" I asked. "Janice and I need to get to work."

We left the diner and returned back to the apartment. When we were inside, Janice and I opened our laptops on the kitchen table while Ryan and Cortland sat in the living room watching television. Janice had a week to adjust to her new living situation, and now it was time for us to begin our business relationship.

I showed her the website and gave her access to the email address. "You can take as many manuscripts as you can at a time, but you need to have a quick turn over rate—my reputation depends on it. You can keep the entire payment as your income, and all the revenue I make from my own projects is mine."

Janice scrolled through the website and saw the books I had already edited in my name. "Christine Dirkson is your client?" she asked incredulously.

"She came to me directly after she became too frustrated working with Carl. She decided she would rather self-publish than subject her work to the demands of someone else."

"Is that why you charge so much?" she asked. "Two thousand dollars per manuscript is insane, Scarlet. I mean, that's an *insane* amount of money."

I opened the email account and browsed through my inbox. "There are already two new people interested in having me complete their work. That's one for you and one for me."

"This is amazing, Scarlet."

"I know," I said. "It's been paying for our rent, food, and utilities for a while. Ryan's business is slow and he's only breaking even every week."

"So, you're supporting him?"

"Only for now."

"Well, we can use my income for rent and other things, too."

I smiled at her. "Don't worry about it, Janice. The arrangement is temporary. When Ryan starts gaining steady business again, I'll stop paying the rent and get a place of my own."

"You're going to move out?" she asked in surprise.

"Yes," I said. "I never planned on staying here forever. I've only been here because I had nowhere else to go."

"Is it because of me?" she asked.

"Of course not, Janice," I said. "But I need my own space and so does Ryan—you and Ryan."

"Well, can I move out with you?" she asked. "I love staying here, but I don't want to mess up this relationship. It might be best if I move out."

"It's up to you," I said. "We can talk about it when the time comes. There is no way to tell how long that will be."

Janice nodded. "I still want to help out, Scarlet. I insist."

"Well, you can help Ryan pay off his old equipment. He is

still in debt from that."

"Of course," she said. "I will. I want to help out as much as possible. We are in this together."

Her generosity made me feel a pang of guilt. I didn't call her for weeks and left her completely alone, wondering what happened to me. She hadn't done anything wrong and I never had the integrity to say anything to her. "I miss this," I whispered.

"I missed my best friend, too."

I smiled at her then looked down at the computer screen. There was a knock on the door but Ryan was on his feet before I could move.

"I got it," he said. Ryan walked to the door and opened it. He stood there for a moment and waited for the visitor to speak. The man was wearing a black suit and was holding a single envelope.

"Is Scarlet Reese available?" he asked without preamble.

"What is this regarding?" Ryan asked.

"Legal affairs."

Ryan turned to me and I walked to the door. When I reached the entranceway, the man stared at me blankly.

"Are you Ms. Reese?" he asked.

I nodded, too anxious to speak. He handed me the envelope and walked away. When he was gone, I shut the door and locked it then ran the envelope through my fingers. Ryan started at it over my shoulder. The corner of the envelope indicated it was from the government. I felt my heart hammer in my chest. I already knew what it contained but I was still frightened.

Cortland and Janice came into the kitchen and stood in front of me, saying nothing as they stared at me, unsure what to do. Ryan remained silent as he stood next to me, waiting for me to open the letter.

I tore open the top and pulled out the single page tucked inside. The black letters of the page jumped out at me, but all I saw was the color red. I skimmed through the notes then dropped my hands to my side.

"I just got served."

Ryan sighed. "When?"

"Next week," I said quietly. "If I don't have thirty percent of the money before the court date, then I'll be sued."

Ryan grabbed his head as he paced through the kitchen. Janice ran her fingers through her hair as she became lost in thought. Cortland stared right at me, like I was about to combust into a million pieces.

"I thought you said you were going to figure this out," Ryan said. "Scarlet—this is serious."

"You think I don't know that?"

Ryan sighed. "What the fuck are we going to do?"

"Nothing," I said. "There is nothing we can do."

Ryan ignored me. "Cortland, can we borrow some money?"

"No," I snapped. "I refuse to take money from friends."

"Why?" Ryan asked.

"I have no idea if I can ever pay him back. I would much

rather steal money from the government than my own friends."

"You do realize that they are going to take you for everything you have?" Ryan snapped.

"Then it's a good thing I don't have anything."

"You have your company," he said. "They are going to take it away from you and sell it."

I dropped the letter on the ground and looked at him. "What?"

Ryan didn't repeat his words. My look of dumbfounded heartbreak was enough to shut him up. Janice crossed her arms over her chest and shifted her weight. The room was silent after Ryan spoke.

"They'll take away my company?" I whispered.

Ryan nodded.

Without thinking, I turned towards the front door, grabbed my coat, and then walked out of the apartment. Cortland and Ryan both stepped towards me, but I held up my hand. "Let me go." Cortland didn't stop and he grabbed my arm. "I said let me go." Cortland released his hand after a moment of hesitation.

I wasn't sure where I was going or what I was doing. I just knew that I had to run. My family was back in the apartment, but I didn't want them—I didn't want anyone. My company was finally a success and it was everything that I dreamed it would be. After all that hard work, I had to give it up. It was being taken away from me and there's nothing I could do about it. The tears fell down my face and made my vision blurry as I walked down the main strip. It was dark outside, and only the lights of the streetlamps guided my way through the night. It wasn't safe to walk around Seattle alone, but I didn't care at that point. Everything that I had worked for was crashing down. Without the income from the company, I couldn't support me and Ryan. He would lose the shop and we would be homeless. I'd promised Janice a job, but now I was about to screw her over.

I made it the pier and stopped when I heard the ocean waves beat against the shore. I leaned over the rail as I looked into the black waves below me. Their white caps couldn't be seen, but I could hear them crash against the beach. The sound of crying seagulls entered my brain, but I didn't listen to it. I felt blind to the world.

A man stopped a few feet away from me and I was suddenly aware of his close proximity. I glanced in his direction and realized that Ryan was watching me, making sure I was safe.

"I can't believe you followed me," I said.

Ryan placed his hands in his jacket pockets and moved closer to me. "I can."

"I want to be alone, Ryan."

"Then pretend I'm not here."

The ocean wind tickled my skin and pulled the strands of hair from my face. The sting of the salty air stung my nostrils and irritated my sinuses. I felt lost and empty.

"What if we change the license to your name?" I asked. "They can't take it away from me if you own it."

Ryan shook his head. "I don't think that will work," he said. "They wouldn't be suing you unless you had something worth suing for. I am sure these lawyers did their research—they know you have the company."

I slammed my hand on the rail and ignored the pain that shot through my arm. "Why is this happening to me?" I asked. "I can't catch a goddamn break." I wasn't just referring to the company, but everything in my life. Sean continued to screw up our relationship even though I believed he was different now, and my life's greatest accomplishment was all a waste. "What's the point?"

"We are going to figure this out, Scarlet."

"Don't say that—it isn't true," I snapped. "You're going to lose the shop because of this—or end up homeless."

"We'll find a way."

I took a deep breath and slowed my breathing. The tears were starting to creep from under my eyes, and I fought them with all the strength I had. Crying would change nothing, and I didn't want to waste my time being pathetic.

"What do we do?" I asked.

"Hopefully, they'll give you an extension. Then we'll leave the apartment and move in with Cortland, pooling our money together until we pay off your loan."

"And what if they don't?" I asked.

Ryan sighed. "We'll deal with that when the time comes."

I backed away from the rail and placed my hands in my

pockets. Ryan stared at me for a moment then his gaze moved to the people walking past us. It was obvious that Ryan felt threatened by the tension in his body.

"Let's go home," he whispered. He grabbed my arm and pulled me from the rail. I could tell by the force of his grip that he wouldn't accept an argument from me. We walked up the street towards the apartment. As we got closer to home, Ryan started to ease up. He placed his arm around me and I rested my head on his shoulder. When we made it back to the apartment, Janice and Cortland were sitting on the couch waiting for us.

"I'm going to bed," I said without looking at them. I walked down the hall and closed my bedroom door behind me. When I was alone with my thoughts, I realized how Sean felt when he learned the truth about Penelope. Reality was too harsh to bear and he turned to an escape, something that I wanted at that moment. But I could never do that. I had a family that I couldn't let down—they needed me.

20

There were a few days before the court date, so I spent that time doing everything I could to not think about it. For the first time, I allowed myself to think about Sean because it distracted my mind from my unavoidable fate. I wanted to tell him about it, but I knew I couldn't. He wasn't in my life anymore.

Janice and I went down to Mega-Shake for a few hours to work on our manuscripts. We were trying to finish up our work as soon as possible so we could collect our payment. If I lost the business, Ryan would have the money to pay rent and take care of the shop for a while.

Janice sat across from me with her laptop opened and we worked together in silence. Sometimes we would ask for a second opinion about a sentence or grammatical issue, and it was convenient having another editor for input.

Her phone kept vibrating all day, indicating she'd received a text message. She always smiled as she read the words on her phone. I rolled my eyes when I watched her. It was Ryan. After a while, she ignored the phone altogether because he continued to message her and it was disrupting her work. Finally, her phone rang and she answered it.

"Yes, I'm still at Mega-Shake with Scarlet." She smiled. "I don't know—soon." Ryan was so hooked on Janice that it was just pathetic. Since he never felt that way about anyone before, I decided not to tease him about it. If he was happy, I was happy. "Okay," she said. "I'll head home now but I do have work to do afterwards." She hung up the phone and started packing her equipment into her bag.

"I'm sorry that my brother is so annoying," I said.

"I think it's sweet." She smiled. "Are you coming, too?"

I shook my head. "I'm going to stay here for a while longer."

"I'll see you at home," she said as she left the restaurant.

I was the only one left inside Mega-Shake. There were no customers on that weeknight, and the workers behind the counter were playing on their cell phones, bored out of their minds. One of the employees was eating a bowl of fries that would just go to waste if it wasn't eaten. I stared at them with a smile on my face then looked back at my computer screen.

The door opened, but I didn't look up to see who entered the shop. The sentence I was reading on my computer was poorly constructed, and I was trying to make it more clear and concise. The table rocked as someone sat across from me. Alarmed, I looked over my laptop and froze when I saw the person on the other side.

I stared at him for a moment before I found my bearings. I was so nervous and surprised that I didn't know how to react. My computer screen was blocking most of his face so I closed it.

"What are you doing here?" I asked.

Sean stared at me with his blue eyes, and I felt hypnotized by the look. Even though I left him and swore that our relationship was over, I still missed him and thought about him every day. I swallowed back those feelings as I looked at him. Nothing had changed.

"I want to say something to you," he said as he leaned forward. "And I don't want you to interrupt me. Okay?"

I nodded.

"I've been thinking about everything and I realized something. Even after everything I did to you, fucking everything up, you still came to me when I hit my lowest point. I know how much I hurt you, and the fact that you helped me speaks louder than words. You are just as in love with me as the first time you realized it, and nothing I do will change that. Since this is how you feel, I think you should give me another chance. I promise I won't hurt you again and I'm yours until you no longer want me." He stared at me and waited for me to speak. The panic was obvious in Sean's eyes, and I knew he was desperate to win me back. When I thought about everything that'd happened, it made me realize that our relationship could never work.

"No."

Sean sighed. "Scarlet—"

"Now it's my turn," I whispered. Sean fell silent. "You still had Penelope's ring the entire time, meaning that you were still waiting for her to come back to you. You've never been over her, and that's fine, but you always wanted her back. You proposed to her when you were still with me. I don't want to be a second choice, Sean. Nothing you say will change that. You were willing to sacrifice everything for her, but you wouldn't even consider moving here to make this relationship work, and now I know why—you were waiting for Penelope."

"That is completely wrong," he argued. "I never proposed to Penelope. She saw the ring on the table and put it on herself. I just didn't tell her to stop. The only reason I didn't move to Seattle is because of my job and my friends—that's it. And I know I would have made the move eventually because I can't live without you. I understand why you feel the way you do, but please give me one more chance to prove you wrong—I promise you won't regret it."

To say that I didn't want to be with Sean would be a lie—I did. But I also knew that I could never look past everything he did. It wasn't that I couldn't forgive him. I just couldn't stand the pain of being less loved than Penelope. Knowing that he didn't propose to Penelope did make me feel better, but I was still hurt that he left me. "I'm sorry that you wasted your time, Sean," I said. "You should go home."

Sean stared at me. "I am home, Scar."

I looked at him. "What do you mean?"

"*You* are home, Scar. I don't know why I didn't realize it before. I've moved to Seattle. My apartment is down the street, fairly close to you and Ryan, and I'm not going back to New York—whether you give me another chance or not. You are going to be in my life—nothing is more important to me."

My tongue was immobile in my mouth. I was speechless. Sean had moved there without me asking him. He gave up his position at the firm, a job he loved, and now he was living in Seattle with me. This was exactly what I wanted from the beginning. "You moved here?"

Sean smiled at me. "Yes."

The seat rocked as I leaned back in my chair. I crossed my arms over my chest and thought for a moment. It wasn't enough. He still picked Penelope over me. He can argue it was for the baby, but I didn't see it that way. I never would.

"Please say something," he whispered.

"That doesn't change anything."

Sean ran his hands through his hair. "I am completely devoted to you in every way. Please, Scarlet, give me another chance. I am the one you want so take me—I won't hurt you again."

I put my laptop into my bag and placed the bag over my shoulder as I walked away from the table. Sean followed me outside.

"Scarlet, just think about it," he begged.

I turned around and looked at him. "It's over, Sean—we're done. I suggest you move back to New York because I'm not going to change my mind." I marched up the street back towards my apartment and I heard Sean following behind me. Night had descended on the city and I knew Sean didn't want me to walk home alone. "I don't need you to protect me, Sean. I can take care of myself."

Sean didn't comment on my words. My bag fell from my shoulder as he took it. He carried it for me up the street. I didn't bother yelling at him since I knew it would accomplish nothing. When we got to the entrance of my building, I stopped.

"I can take it from here."

Sean opened the door and walked into the building. I took a deep breath then followed him. We got into the elevator and rode it up to the fifth floor. I felt Sean staring at me as we stood next to each other. His fingers brushed mine, but I pulled them away.

When the doors opened, I immediately stepped out and headed down the hallway to my apartment. Sean followed behind me without saying anything. When we got to my door, I took my keys out of my pocket and inserted them into the lock.

"Good night, Sean," I said. "Have a safe trip back."

Sean grabbed my arm and pulled me to him. "You kissed me, Scarlet. The tears were falling from your eyes like a river. Admit it—you love me. I'm not going to give up on you so you may as well get used to it." Sean grabbed my face and kissed me. Initially, I tried to pull away, but he wouldn't release his grip on me. I gave into the moment and returned his kiss with passion, running my hands through his hair while I felt him slide his hands down my back. Logical thought eventually returned to me, and I pushed him away.

"Don't ever touch me like that again," I yelled.

Sean's face fell as he listened to me.

"Kissing me isn't going to fix everything, Sean, and neither is moving here. You fucked everything up and it can't be undone. We are through, Sean—done."

The front door opened and Ryan stared at us for a moment. "Is everything okay?"

"Get rid of him," I said as I walked into the apartment.

Ryan turned back to Sean. "Come in," he said.

Furious, I turned back to Ryan and held my hand up to Sean. "I said get rid of him. I don't want to see him, Ryan. He just kissed me when I didn't want it. If anything, you should beat the shit out of him."

Ryan stared at me for a moment. "Fine," he said. He walked outside and shut the door behind him, standing with Sean in the hallway.

"You have to be kidding me," I said under my breath. I dropped my bag on the table and Janice flinched at my aggression. She didn't say anything and I was happy that she wasn't dumping a bunch of questions on me. I was shocked that Sean had moved to Seattle to be with me. My lips still tingled from the kiss that we shared in the hallway, but I forced the thought from my mind. It couldn't happen again.

Twenty minutes later, Ryan came back into the apartment and closed the door behind him. Sean didn't follow him inside, and I was relieved that he wasn't coming into the room. I glared at Ryan.

"What were you talking about?" I asked.

"Sports," he said.

"Tell me."

"I'm starting to get irritated with you."

"What did I do?" I asked incredulously.

"Sean moved here for you—*moved*. Give him another chance, Scarlet. What else can the guy do to prove himself?"

"He can't undo what he did."

"I'm aware of that," he snapped. "But he's doing everything he can to get you back."

"You even told me he didn't deserve a second chance," I said. "Why are you taking his side? You are supposed to protect me."

"That was before—he made an effort," he said quietly. "Sean has proven his sincerity to you. I don't want you to regret this later when Sean moves on and it's too late. I don't want you to be in a relationship with a reasonable guy that doesn't make you happy. Just give him one more chance."

"This conversation is over."

"Scarlet—"

"Drop it."

Ryan sighed as he stared at me. He turned to Janice. "Let's go to bed." He turned and walked down the hallway.

Janice looked at me. "Do you want to talk about it?"

"No."

"I agree with Ryan."

"Good for you."

"Why don't—"

"Just go to bed, Janice."

Her eyes widened in offense at my quick words. The skin of her lips stretched tight as she grabbed her stuff and looked away. She grabbed her belongings and disappeared from the room, leaving me alone in the kitchen. When the late hours of night descended, I finally went to bed.

21

"You are playing ball with us today," Ryan said as he came into the living room in his gym clothes with a basketball tucked under his arm. He made himself a cup of coffee then looked at me while he drank from it. I was still staring at my computer screen like I wasn't listening. "Did you hear me?"

"Yes."

"Then go get dressed."

"I'm going to stay here."

"You need to get out of the house and away from the screen. Come on. Cortland will be here soon."

"What about Janice?"

"She says she's too tired. We were up late last night." He smiled.

I sighed. I felt lethargic from the lack of exercise and I realized I should take a break from my work. It was moving as slow as a snail anyway. "Fine," I said as I walked down the hallway.

I returned a few moments later wearing my workout clothes. Cortland was sitting at the kitchen table.

"I was wondering when you were going to be done." He smiled. "We are going to the courts—not the Grammys."

"Save your trash talk for the court." I smiled. Ryan and

Cortland didn't mention Sean and I was grateful for the silence. The three of us walked a few blocks up the street until we made it to the basketball courts. There was no one there except for a guy sitting on the benches. The man stood up when we approached, and when he came closer, I realized it was Sean.

I glared at Ryan. "You're such an ass."

Ryan ignored me. "What are the odds?" he said with a surprised voice.

"I had no idea Sean was going to be here," Cortland added. "Now the teams will be even."

They were sounding guiltier by the minute. "I hate you both," I mumbled. I crossed my arms over my chest and didn't look at Sean. When he walked over to us, he looked at me, but didn't speak.

"Let's play two on two," Ryan said.

"I'm on Cortland's team," I said quickly as I walked over to him.

Cortland and Ryan shared an awkward look. "Well, I already said I would be on Ryan's team," Cortland said as he walked away. "We decided that earlier."

I placed my hands on my hips. "I thought you didn't know Sean was going to be here?"

They both looked dumbfounded, caught in their lie.

Sean came next to me. "I would love to be on your team," he said. "We work well together."

I ignored him and walked away. Ryan was dribbling the

ball and I stole it from him, running up the court and making a basket. Ryan stole the ball and threw it to Cortland, but Sean stole the ball and passed it to me. I made another basket. Sean and I could anticipate what the other would do before we even did it, making us a good team. As much as I hated to admit it, I knew it was true. After we played for a while, I stopped thinking about the uncomfortable situation between Sean and I, and just focused on playing the game. When the game ended an hour later, Ryan and Cortland did their usual victory dance on the court and I rolled my eyes at them.

"We'll win next time," Sean said as he stood next to me.

"There won't be a next time, Sean."

Cortland and Ryan came over to us and we started to walk down the street to Mega-Shake. I looked at Sean. "Don't you have somewhere to be?" I said in an ugly voice. I didn't want Sean hanging out with my family. He gave up that right when he betrayed me.

"No," Cortland said for him. "I already asked."

I fell silent as we walked to the restaurant. I was furious at both Ryan and Cortland for orchestrating this, making Sean and I spend time together in the hope that our love would rekindle. When we got to the restaurant, we washed our hands and ordered our food before we sat down in our usual booth. Sean sat directly across from me, so I was forced to meet his gaze.

I didn't speak while we ate and just listened to the men talk. Sean was staring at me the entire time, and I was growing irritated with the look. I was more irritated that Ryan's plan was working, and I felt the spasm of my heart when I looked at Sean. I missed him.

"How is your company doing?" Sean asked.

I didn't respond to his question because of the drama I was in at that moment. It wasn't going to be mine in a few days.

"Are you ignoring him now?" Ryan asked.

I glared at him before I looked at Sean. "It's fine," I said. "But I'm selling it. I already put the offer online."

"What?" Ryan interjected. "When were you planning on telling me this?"

"Now," I said.

"Why?" Ryan asked.

"I can pay back the minimum amount on the loan and I'll have some money left over. I'll find a job doing something else." When I looked at Ryan, he was staring at Sean and their eyes were locked. Sean nodded slightly and Ryan seemed to calm down. I didn't understand what the interaction meant.

"Sell it after they take you to court," Ryan said. "You aren't sure if you will even have to sell it yet. Don't jump the gun."

"It's my company. I'll do whatever I think is best."

Ryan sighed. "Stop being a brat because I brought Sean along today. I'm just trying to do what's best for you."

"Well, you aren't doing what's best for Sean," I snapped. "You're giving him false hope by supporting this. He's just going to get hurt."

"Then give him another chance," Ryan said.

"I already said no."

Ryan glared at me. "You're being stupid."

"Sean and I are never getting back together. He and I already discussed this last night. Both of you are wasting your time." I stopped eating my food because I'd lost my appetite. "I am ready to move on and start seeing other people."

"You're full of it," Ryan snapped.

"Then set me up with someone," I said. "Hook me up with one of your friends."

Sean's face fell as he listened to my words. He stopped eating and pushed his food away, suddenly losing any interest in eating.

"Stop being a bitch, Scar," Ryan said.

I turned to Cortland. "Do you have any single friends?"

"You made your point," Sean whispered. "I get it."

I fell silent. Ryan glared at me in anger, and Cortland drank his soda without looking at us. I felt horrible for hurting Sean by saying I would consider dating other guys, especially since it was a lie, but I wanted to make it clear that we were over. Ryan and Cortland were trying to encourage his pursuit of the relationship, but I needed to shut it down.

We got up and threw our trash away then left the restaurant. Sean started walking with us back to the apartment and I stared at him.

"Go home, Sean," I said. "You aren't welcome here."

Sean took a deep breath. "You belong with me, Scar. Please don't do this."

I felt the tears fall from my eyes. "No, I deserve someone better than you. I don't want to be with someone that I can't trust. You claim that you love me but you've never done anything to prove it—you only show me otherwise. I don't know how much clearer I have to make it. WE ARE OVER! I DON'T WANT YOU, SEAN. NOW LEAVE ME ALONE." Sean stepped back as I yelled in his face. The redness around his eyes showed the tears that were underneath the surface. He dropped his gaze and looked at the sidewalk. "DO YOU FINALLY GET IT? I WANT TO FIND SOMEONE BETTER THAN YOU. YOU DON'T DESERVE ME!" I felt a hand pull my arm.

"That's enough, Scar," Ryan said to me. "Back off. Sean gets it."

A tear fell down Sean's cheek and was followed by another one. I stared at him until he looked away. "Okay," he whispered. "I'll leave you alone." Sean turned around and walked up the street, the opposite way of the apartment, and he never turned around. When I was sure that he wasn't coming back, I started walking back to our apartment with Cortland and Ryan beside me. They didn't say anything for a long time.

"That was cold, Scar," Ryan said.

"Shut up, Ryan."

He fell silent until we got back to the apartment. I grabbed my laptop from the kitchen table and was going to carry it into my bedroom when Ryan stopped me.

"You should apologize to him, Scar. What you did was fucked up."

I almost slammed my laptop to the ground. I placed it on the table then pushed Ryan back. "No, what you did was fucked up, Ryan. If you hadn't encouraged him to pursue me, I wouldn't have had to break his heart like that. You could have just left it alone." I grabbed my laptop and walked around him.

"You're going to regret this, Scar."

I went into my bedroom, slamming the door behind me.

22

Sean didn't come around for the next three days. I didn't see him at the apartment and he didn't make a surprise appearance at Mega-Shake. The last words I said to him on the street had the desired effect. Sean finally understood that we were over—done. I wondered if he'd moved back to New York yet—I hoped he did.

The closer the court date came, the more nervous I became. I got a few offers on my company but none of them were willing to pay the price I asked for. Ryan said I shouldn't sell it anyway until I found out what was going to happen at my court meeting, and I agreed. I just wanted to see if I had any reasonable offers.

The days passed by quicker than they normally would because I was dreading the passage of time. The court date was just a day away and I hadn't planned anything for the event. Ryan and I didn't have the money for a lawyer, so I was defending myself. I didn't see the point in preparing for it. I was guilty.

Janice and I were sitting at the kitchen table when Ryan walked into the apartment with the mail tucked under his arm. No one had spoken of Sean since the argument we had earlier in the week, and I was glad everyone had given up on the idea of Sean and I getting back together. Ryan sorted through the mail and gave me my stack of letters. I went through the pile and found a letter from the government, reminding me of my court date the following afternoon. I tossed the letter in the trash and grabbed the next envelope.

The letter I held was from a private law firm in Seattle. I stared at it for a moment before I opened it. When I read through the letter, I stood up in surprise, unable to sit any longer. Ryan stared at me without saying anything, waiting for me to speak.

The letter stated that my father's will had been modified due to new legal documentation and that I had inherited money from his stated will. My hands shook as I read the letter. I looked up at Ryan and saw that he was holding the same letter, except he hadn't opened his yet. I looked in the envelope and found a check inside. I screamed when I read the amount.

"How much is it?" Ryan said as he tore open his letter. He dropped the letter on the ground and stared at the check. His eyes widened in surprise. "Holy fucking shit," he yelled.

I was speechless. I stared at the amount again and felt dizzy with vertigo. "Dad left us almost two million dollars?" I asked incredulously. "I can't believe this is happening. And right before I lost my company. What are the odds?"

Ryan didn't respond to my statement. He sat down and started to breathe slowly, controlling the enthusiasm and shock that was coursing through his body. "I can't believe this is happening," he whispered.

"Now we don't have to worry about the shop anymore," I said happily. "I can move out and continue my company." I wrapped my arms around my brother and squeezed him tightly.

"That bitch got what she deserved. I bet she's furious right now."

"I hope she is." Ryan smiled.

Ryan and I held each other for a moment, and I let myself ride the wave of happiness. My mother did everything she could to keep my inheritance away from me, but somehow the money made its way back to me—exactly as my father intended.

"Now I can write a check and be done with this student loan fiasco," I said happily. "I don't even have to go to court."

Ryan nodded. "We both deserve this," he said.

"I know we do."

"So what are you guys going to buy first?" Janice asked with a smile. "I like cars."

Ryan and I both laughed. "I think I'm going to save it," I said. "Just get a comfortable apartment and continue my company."

"I don't think I'm going to change my lifestyle either," he said. "A million dollars isn't much."

"Wow," Janice said sarcastically. "You guys are just so adventurous."

I laughed. "I think Ryan and I are both ready for a peaceful life." Ryan nodded. "This is so random. I don't even know how this came about."

Ryan sighed and looked at me. "I need to tell you something, Scar."

I stared at him for a moment. "It was you?" I asked. "You did all of this?"

Ryan shook his head. "No, Sean did."

"What?" I asked as I stepped back. "He went behind my back and pried into my family affairs?"

"I asked him to," Ryan said quickly. "You told me to drop it, but I refused to do it. We both deserved this money, and I was going to fight for it, but I didn't understand how to do any of it. That's why I turned to Sean. He did everything. I just told him to do it. I wasn't planning on telling you, but in light of recent events, I think you should know."

"Why does it matter?"

Ryan shook his head. "Sean has always been there for you, Scar. He was working on this before he even came back to you. And when he was with Penelope, he was still pursuing it. He beat up your boss, moved here, and now this. If this doesn't warrant him a second chance, I don't know what does."

I sighed. "That's why you were pushing for him this whole time?"

"Yes," he said. "If you still don't want to be with him, which I think is idiotic, that's fine, but you should at least talk to him and tell him how much you appreciate what he did. It's because of him that all our problems are solved. You owe him at least that."

"Why didn't Sean tell me?"

"I asked him not to," Ryan explained. "He kept his word to me even though he could have used it to get you back. He's loyal, Scar. That's another reason why he deserves another chance. He

210

did all this work knowing you would never know he did it for you."

I stared at the check in my hands and realized Ryan was right. Sean must have worked so hard on securing this money for me, and he never once mentioned it. Even if I didn't want to be with him, he still deserved my gratitude and acknowledgment. I placed the check on the table and walked to the door. "I'll be back in a little while."

Ryan smiled at me. "Take all the time you need."

When I arrived at Mega-Shake, I called Sean with shaky hands. The phone rang a few times before he answered it.

"Hello?"

"Hey," I said.

Sean was silent for a moment, unsure of what to say because he didn't know why I was calling. "Are you okay?"

"I'm fine," I said. "Can you meet me at Mega-Shake?"

"I'll be there soon," he said. I hung up the phone and returned it to my pocket. I waited for him in our usual booth by the window. My heart was hammering in my chest as I watched for Sean through the window. Finally, I saw him coming up the sidewalk and my heart nearly exploded at the sight of him. He came into the restaurant and sat down across from me. His face was somber and calm, but the lines of depression could be seen around his eyes. His frame wasn't as straight as it was before, and I could tell he was reliving our last conversation behind his eyes. It was obvious how much I hurt him. He was uncomfortable just from sitting across me.

"Hey," I said.

Sean nodded, but didn't speak. The guilt started to course through me as I looked at him. I was responsible for all of his pain.

"I wanted to talk to you."

Sean still didn't say anything.

"I wanted to thank you for what you did for Ryan and I—researching my father's will and getting us that money. It means a lot to me that you did that."

"I don't know what you're talking about," he said without looking at me.

"Ryan already told me it was you."

Sean finally looked at me. "You aren't mad?"

"No," I said. "I'm—touched that you did that for me. I was going to lose my company, and now I finally have retribution against my mother for keeping my money for all these years. Her greed cost her more than if she had just paid me to begin with."

"That bitch got what she deserved," Sean said as he put his hands in his pockets and leaned back against the seat. His eyes still looked at everything but me.

"Thank you, Sean."

"You're welcome," he whispered. We were silent for a moment and I couldn't think of anything else to say. I'd already told him how much I appreciated what he did, and Sean was looking more uncomfortable by the minute. I could tell that he wanted to get away from me as soon as possible. "Are we done

212

here?"

I thought for a moment. "Yes," I whispered.

Sean nodded and got up, leaving me sitting alone in the restaurant as he walked out the door without saying goodbye. I felt my heart fall as I watched him go, knowing how much I still loved him and wanted him. As I watched him leave my view from the windows, I realized that Sean had proven his love for me many times, but I was so blindsided by the wrong things that he did that I didn't notice or value his deeds. The idea of dating other men sounded repulsive when there was only one guy that I wanted. Now Sean was absolutely in love with me and he was mine if I wanted him. Perhaps I should give him another chance.

I got up from my seat and left the restaurant. Sean was walking down the street when I got outside and I shouted to him.

"Sean!"

He stopped and turned around, seeing me standing outside of Mega-Shake. After a moment of hesitation, he walked back to me with his hands in the pockets of his jacket. "What?" he asked when he stopped in front of me.

I stared at him for a moment. His eyes looked dark in despair and his lips looked colorless and dead, like the blood was draining from his body. I didn't know what to say, and I felt the words leave my mind.

"What?" he asked again.

"I'm sorry about everything."

Sean sighed. "Please don't be."

"Does your offer still stand?"

"What offer?" he asked.

"That you would always be there if I changed my mind?" I crossed my arms over my chest while I looked at him. He was so cold and distant that I wasn't sure if he still wanted me. I had hurt him so viciously a few days earlier. I didn't blame him if he felt differently.

Sean dropped his hands to his side and a smile stretched on his lips. He stepped towards me and pressed his forehead against mine. I felt my heart quicken in my chest. "Yes," he said.

"I'm sorry," I whispered.

"I'm sorry too," he said. He wrapped his arms around my waist and held me to his chest. "Are you giving me another chance?"

"Forever and Always."

He smiled at me. "I promise it will only take one." Sean pressed his lips against mine and kissed me gently. I felt the tears fall from my eyes as I wrapped my arms around his neck and pulled him closer to me. Sean's tears dripped onto my face while we kissed. People were walking past us as they moved up the street but we were oblivious to everything going on around us. Sean pulled away from me.

"I love you."

"I love you, too."

Sean sighed as he pressed his head against mine. "I thought I lost you."

"No," I said. "And you'll never have to worry about it."

"Thank you for giving me another chance."

"A real chance."

"I don't deserve you," Sean said with a smile.

"It's okay. I don't deserve you either."

Sean laughed. "So you are my hot piece of ass girlfriend again?"

"Yes, and I better stay that way."

"We won't have a problem there."

Sean grabbed my hand and we walked back to the apartment at a slow pace. When we were in the elevator, Sean kissed my cheek as he wrapped his arms around me, and when the doors opened, an old couple was staring at us. We both ignored them as we left the elevator and walked down the hallway to the apartment.

When we were inside, Janice and Ryan were sitting on the couch with their backs to us. Sean cleared his throat, and Ryan turned his head at the sound. His mouth stretched into a smile when he saw our joined hands. He got up and started clapping loudly and Janice did the same.

"About fucking time," Ryan said as he came over to us. He shook hands with Sean and nodded to him. "Don't fuck this up again," he said. "You have no idea how many times I had to argue with this brat for you."

Sean laughed. "I'm sorry about that," he said. "I know how annoying she can be. And don't worry—I got this."

"So, you are already making fun of me with my brother?" I asked incredulously. "That didn't last long."

Sean kissed my head. "Get over it."

I rolled my eyes.

"Thank you for everything, Sean," Ryan said. "You saved our asses."

Sean nodded. "That's what family is for," he said with a shrug.

"Let's go back to your apartment," I said as I wrapped my arms around his neck and pulled him close, rubbing my nose against his.

"I'm standing right here," Ryan said sarcastically.

"What's your point?" I said as I started kissing Sean.

"That's gross," he said.

"I hear you and Janice in the middle of the night," I snapped.

"That's different."

"No, it isn't."

"Yes, I'm your older brother—I'm a man."

"You are such a sexist pig," I said as I grabbed Sean's hand and pulled him towards the door. "I'm going to Sean's. I probably won't be home for several days." We walked out the door and took a cab to Sean's apartment up the street.

When we got inside the apartment, I looked around at all the new furniture and decorations in his place. I assumed he let Penelope keep all of his old stuff in his apartment in New York.

"You have a nice place," I said as I looked around.

"Thank you," he said as he came up behind me. I turned around and started kissing him in the living room, running my hands through his hair and down to his chest. I started to unbutton his shirt when he grabbed my hands and stopped me.

"Just because we're in my apartment doesn't mean I'm going to sleep with you."

"You've got to be kidding me," I said. "We've already slept together. I don't want to wait."

"I'm sorry." He sighed. "But it's not going to happen."

"You are killing me."

"I know." He sighed. "I'm anxious too."

"Do you not want me?" I asked sadly.

"That's a stupid question and you know it," he said. "Our sex was amazing. Of course I want to do it again."

"Why are you being such a prude? That isn't who you are. I bet you can't even count the number of girls you've slept with."

"You're right," he said. "And that's because they didn't mean anything."

My eyes softened at his words.

I know how frustrated you were last time, but I have to do this. I want you to trust me before I make love to you. Even though you took me back, I know you're still hurting."

I sighed. "Sean, let's move on."

He shook his head. "I'm sorry. I have to do this. I don't feel like I deserve to make love to you. Let me prove myself."

"You are so annoying," I said as I shook my head.

He smiled. "I know."

"Can we do other stuff?"

He sighed. "I don't think so," he said. "It will be too hard for me to stop."

"I seriously want to kill you," I said.

Sean laughed. "You really want me."

"I think that's obvious." I smiled. "I practically had to rape you last time. And it was amazing, so amazing that haven't stopped thinking about it since. I want to do it again."

"We can only kiss—with our clothes on."

"I hate you."

Sean kissed me. "I love you," he said. "Now let me show you something." He grabbed my hand and took me down the hallway to a doorway. When he opened it, he let me walk inside first. There was a large wooden desk in the middle of the room with bookshelves on the walls. There were pictures of us on the desk, along with a filing cabinet for my manuscripts.

"I thought this could be your office," he said.

I stared at the room then looked back at him. "It's amazing," I said.

"Now let me show you this," he said as he walked into his bedroom. He opened his walk-in closet and showed me the empty part of the storage area, which took up over half of the closet. "I know how much crap you have." He smiled. Then, he walked over to one of the dressers and pulled open the drawers. "This is all for you."

"Do you want me to move in?" I asked.

"Whenever you're ready," he said.

I walked over to him and wrapped my arms around him. "I love it," I said as I kissed him.

"Good," he said as he kissed me back. I pushed him on top of the bed and climbed on top of him, kissing him passionately as I ran my hands through his hair. Sean moaned when I slipped my tongue in his mouth then he rolled over on top of me, running his hand down my legs. After a moment, he pulled away. "It isn't going to work, Scarlet, but nice try."

I pulled off my shirt then tossed it on the ground. "I want you."

He sighed. "I know."

I unbuttoned my pants and slipped them off. "Please."

He leaned over me then removed my underwear and bra. I was so happy that I wore down his defenses and won. I reached for his shirt but he wouldn't let me remove it. He pulled me to the edge of the bed then kneeled on the floor. I knew what he was going to do.

"I want to make love, Sean."

"No."

"Then fuck me."

He swallowed the lump in his throat. "I can't do that either. But I want to please you. Don't worry, I'll still make you come every night." As soon as his tongue licked my clit, I was lost to him. I wanted to say no, that it wasn't fair to him, but my hormones won the battle of logical thought. He rubbed my clit then he inserted his fingers within me and made me experience a new realm of pleasure. He kissed my thighs as he swirled his fingers around me. I gripped his hair as he made me shake. He rose to a stand and leaned over me, still fingering me. I opened my legs further apart, so he could maneuver deeper.

"Come for me, babe."

"I am."

"Come on." He kissed my lips and I gripped his back with sharp nails. Luckily, he still had his shirt on.

I felt the explosion hit me. "I'm coming."

"I love you."

"Sean." I moaned. "Babe."

"I love you more than anything."

"Sean, I love you too."

My orgasm ended and I felt the air return to my lungs. Sean pulled his fingers out of me then kissed me gently. I waited for him to remove his pants but he didn't. He sat next to me on the bed.

He got off me and I sighed. "You must be gay."

"Or just madly in love."

"No," I said. "You're gay."

Sean laughed. "I'll prove you wrong eventually."

"Can we still sleep together?" I asked.

"I assumed we would tonight—fully dressed, of course."

"We'll see," I said. "There are things I can do that will

make you lose control. You won't be able to be such a gentleman."

Sean walked back to me and leaned over me. "I don't think you understand how hard this is for me," he said. "Please respect my wishes and don't try to seduce me. You're right—I won't be able to resist you—so please don't compromise me. I am only doing this because I love you—that's it."

I stared at the sincerity in his eyes and immediately felt guilty for deciding to test his limits. I wanted to make love to Sean, but I knew this was important to him. If he didn't care about me like any other girl, then he would sleep with me, but since he actually loved me, he wouldn't. I grabbed his face and kissed him gently. "I won't," I said. "I'm sorry I was being such a slut."

Sean laughed loudly then hugged me. "Thank you," he said. "After we get past this, you can be as much of a slut as you want. In fact, a bigger slut is always better."

"But only for you, right?"

"Yes," he said. "Only for me.

Epilogue

Six months later, Sean officially asked me to move in with him. While I was happy that he decided we were ready for this new stage in our relationship, I was also confused. We still hadn't slept together. Against my strong desire for the love of life, I respected his wishes and did the best I could not compromise him by making a sexual advance on him. We had gotten carried away a few times when I slept over, but one of us would stop our actions before they escalated into something more. There were times when I knew Sean had no control over his emotions, and he would have slept with me if I didn't calm him down by stopping him. More often, it was me that lost control and crossed the lines that Sean had drawn. So, when he asked me to move in, I assumed that meant Sean knew I was ready for a physical relationship.

When I told Ryan I was moving, he seemed genuinely happy about it. Our apartment was only a few blocks from his, so we would still see each other on a regular basis. Janice was still living with him and Ryan seemed happier than ever. I suspected he was going to propose soon, but he hadn't said anything to me. I knew he would tell me when he decided.

Cortland helped us move my belongings in his car, which didn't take very many trips since I didn't own very many things. The furniture in my room was already there when I arrived.

Cortland helped me carry my belongings into the living room and we set the boxes wherever there was space available.

"Let's grab some lunch," Cortland said to both of us.

I had no interest in spending time with Cortland now that I knew Sean was willing to take our relationship to the next level, but Sean answered before I could respond.

"I have some work to do, but take Scarlet with you. I'll be finished by the time you get back."

I glared at him. "You have work to do *now*?"

"Yes." He smiled as he kissed me on the head. "Have fun."

Cortland walked out the door and I followed him. We got in the car and drove to the same deli we went to many months earlier. When we were eating our food, Cortland wiped his mouth and spoke.

"He still hasn't given it up?" he asked with a smile.

"You can tell?"

He laughed. "The sexual frustration is leaking out of your pores right now. I can see it."

"Thanks."

"That's rough. I don't think I could stay with a girl if she made me wait that long. I'm glad Monnique was classy, but not too classy."

"How are you two?"

"Great," he said. "I'm going to ask her to move in."

"That's exciting."

"I know," he said. "I would propose, but I don't think she's ready. I want this relationship to move forward, but I don't want to rush her. I think moving in together is a good step."

"I do too."

"Now that you're moving in, he'll put out," he said. "Don't worry about it."

"He better," I said. "Otherwise I'm going to rape him."

Cortland laughed. "I don't think it's possible for you to rape anyone."

"I feel like it sometimes," I said. "How he can wait this long is beyond my comprehension."

"I think he is just trying to prove himself," he said. "I have to give him recognition for that. He is determined to make this relationship a success."

I finished my food and pushed it away. Cortland was already done, but he was waiting for me to finish.

"Are you ready?" he asked.

"Yes," I said. "I am going to seduce Sean as soon as I get home."

Cortland laughed as he grabbed our trash and threw it away. "I have a feeling that you are going to be successful," he said. "If not, the guy is gay."

Cortland opened the door for me and we drove back to the apartment.

"He is definitely *not* gay," I said. "He is just determined."

"Well, he's got some powerful motivation." He stopped at a red light then turned left. "Did you hear about Carl?"

"What about him?" I asked with interest.

"Apparently, not only are some of the other women from the office coming forward and suing him, but the company is as well. I have a feeling you are going to get more money out of this."

"I don't care about that," I said.

"Well, he's going to be in jail for a long time, if that makes your day."

I smiled. "It does."

"And you know what Sean told me?"

I raised an eyebrow. He told me everything. "What?"

"Penelope had her baby."

Now I knew why he didn't mention it. "Oh."

"But guess who she tricked into marrying her?"

I had no idea. "Who?"

"Brian." He started laughing. "Man, that guy is an idiot."

I started laughing hysterically. "He was never very bright."

We got out of the car and Cortland walked me to the door. When I got my key in the lock, he walked away. "Good luck with the art of seduction," he said over his shoulder.

"Thanks." I laughed.

When I walked into the living room, Sean wasn't there. All the lights were out like he hadn't been in the room the whole time.

"I'm in the bedroom," Sean yelled down the hall.

I followed his voice and walked down the hall until I reached the bedroom. I saw the flickering lights and the dancing shadows as I walked inside. There were white candles that covered every surface in the bedroom, and the dim light from their wicks made the room glow by its own luminescence. White rose pedals were sprinkled on the ground and on top of the bed, making it the most romantic sight I've ever seen. Sean stepped out of the corner and stood in front of me.

"I want this to be perfect," he said as he pressed his forehead against mine.

"It's beautiful, Sean."

Sean was holding a large yellow envelope in his hands. "I want you to open this."

I stared at the package for a moment before I opened it. It was a bound manuscript.

"Read it to me," he said.

"*What*?"

"I want to hear it," he said. "It looks interesting. And I love the sound of your voice."

Sean had never taken an interest in my work. He was interested simply because it was my passion, but he never picked up manuscripts and read them for pleasure. I opened the first page and read the acknowledgement. *For Scarlet*, it read. I thought it was a weird coincidence, but I didn't overthink it.

I opened the first page and began to read. "I'm not really a writer," I said. "I just say what I think and put in on the page, destroying a perfectly beautiful and pure piece of paper and demolishing it with my thoughts, which are always conflicted and confusing. And most of the time, I don't have anything important to say—or anything at all.

"But this is the one instance that I do. You see, I'm a bit of an asshole, a complete dickhead most of the time, but I am also incredibly loyal and loving to those who deserve it—for the most part. My story starts a few months in the past, when I was living a blind and pathetic existence. I had the love of a beautiful woman— or so I thought—I had money, food, and water. Life was good. But then this bitch betrayed me and sent me to the brink with rage. No one cared about the pain I was in, and most of the time people didn't even notice how hurt I was, but there was one person who did care because she loved me—her name is Scarlet." My voice caught when I read this line. I looked at Sean and he smiled to me. He nodded towards me, encouraging me to continue.

"But, of course, I was a complete jerk—this is where the asshole and dickhead part comes into play—and I used her. She was my best friend, but I slept with her, disregarding her feelings and emotions. This girl was madly in love with me, would do anything for me—she would even die for me—but I was so blind I didn't even notice. I was so self-absorbed that I didn't even care. It was only when I kissed her—thinking of someone else—did I notice how beautiful she was. The feel of her lips on mine sent shivers down my spine, giving me a rush like I never had before. I never felt that way with anyone. Why didn't I notice it then?

"No. I continued to be a fucking idiot. I broke her heart and crushed her into pieces, and instead of comforting her when she needed me most, when the jerk at her office was assaulting her, I fucked her friend—someone I didn't even care for—rather than confront my true feelings for the most amazing woman in the world—Scarlet. All I had to do was talk to her, my best friend, and I tell her what I was thinking and how I was feeling, but no, I decided to be an idiot—which I tend to be most of the time.

"I pushed her away, and what was worse, I let her go. I let Scarlet go. I knew I loved her. It was as obvious as a colored painting. Everything I saw reminded me of her, from the flowers in the park, to the weights at the gym, and even that weird ink stain on my paper that slightly resembled her, but not really. It took me so long to realize what I wanted—Scarlet. Yes, I was broken hearted over someone else, someone that I thought I wanted to spend my life with, but in the end, my thoughts were focused on the fire in my soul—the girl of my dreams.

"I went after her and it was amazing. The sex was incredible—this heathen was a fireball in bed—and that's putting it lightly." I stopped and laughed at that part. Sean smiled at me when he saw me giggle. I continued reading. "I loved seeing her love for me in her eyes. They shined like beacons in the lighthouses that called lost ships to shore, beckoning them to where they belong. Just the way she touched my face when she kissed me made me realize I belonged to her—and her alone. The idea of anyone else was unthinkable. What the fuck took me so long? Saying goodbye to her at the airport was like saying goodbye to summer every year, preparing for the harsh snow storms that destroyed our houses and land. I never wanted to leave.

"This is where it went wrong. The whore who betrayed, the one I wanted to marry, came to me and begged me to take her back. I couldn't deny the feelings in my heart. She had been the one. I thought she still might be and now she claimed to be carrying my baby. I had to be there for my kid, make sure he had a proper family. I was stupid and idiotic, giving this girl another chance when I never should have. I was losing Scarlet, trading in a beautiful stallion for a mere mule, but I wasn't thinking clearly—I wasn't thinking straight. I was obviously out of my mind. I wanted Scarlet—she was the one. Stop! What the fuck am I doing?

"I did it. I ended it with her, the love of my life, the apple of my eye, the skip in my step, but only because I didn't realize that's what she was. For some inexplicable, illogical reason, I actually thought—imagined—that I was doing the right thing. That somehow choosing the whore was the right choice, even though my Scarlet is perfect in every way. Not only is she beautiful with a jaw-dropping physique, exquisite tits, and legs that make me want to fuck her just by looking at them, but she is the most wonderful girl in the world. She loves me more than any other—including my parents and my family. This girl would die for me and be happy to do it. She watches baseball and gets into it more than I do, and this hot chick can eat a whole pizza by herself and then ask if I want ice cream. She understands when to push me and other times when to hold back. Scarlet completes me in every way. What the fuck am I doing? Don't do this, Sean! Why the fuck are you doing this? You are going the wrong fucking way.

"And then the ultimate betrayal came. I thought the whore and I were together—back to where we were—but it wasn't right. Everything was different—nothing was the same. The sex was passionless and empty. The feel of her lips was cold and hard, like kissing a desiccated corpse in the desert. She didn't talk to me. She didn't ask me about my day. She would rather watch the Real Housewives than watch a nature show like Scarlet and I did. She went down on me, but only because I asked her to. It wasn't what I wanted. She wasn't my Scarlet. That was the moment I knew—I just made the biggest mistake of my life. Scarlet was the one—she had always been. I went the wrong way.

"This is the darkest part. I found old pain killers in my cabinet and started mixing them with rum. It was enough at first, but then I need more. I needed something else. Scarlet was the drug I needed. I needed her to pull me out. She was the only thing that could. But I didn't deserve her. I was a fucking jackass that deserved to die. She shouldn't even come to my funeral. I didn't blame her if she didn't show." I felt the tears behind my eyes when I read on, remembering how much pain he had been in. He was half-alive, mostly dead, and so weak. I knew how much he needed me at that moment, and even then, I wanted to take him back, but I knew I couldn't. Now I wished I had. "It wasn't the loss of Penelope that drove me into that stage of utter confusion and the blackness of an abyss. It was the loss of My Scarlet—she was everything to me. Why did it take me so long to figure it out? And why did it have to be when I was so high that I couldn't tell the ceiling from the floor? Or my nose from my anus? I continued to fall, hoping that death would catch me.

"Then things got better. My Scarlet came to me and nursed me back to health. She shouldn't have come but I was so happy that she did. A part of me knew she would. The feel of her touch helped me live again, knowing she still loved me, and maybe wanted me. I knew how much I hurt her when I listened to her cry. Why the fuck did I do this to her? What the fuck is wrong with me? Stop Sean!

"The cab pulled down the street and I knew my heart was in the backseat of that cab, sitting next to Scarlet as she returned home—Scarlet was *mine*. She had always been mine. I had to go back to her. I had to try. I didn't deserve her, but I would do anything to prove my love for that girl—prove that I was a changed man—that I could be *her* Sean. I could make it right if I just had one more chance—just one more.

"Scarlet screamed at me with tears in her eyes and I knew how much she hated me. She didn't want me anymore—we were done. I went back to my apartment and stayed in bed for days, doing nothing but waiting for death to take me.

"Only in the midst of a tragedy did I get what I want—something I would never want. Scarlet had been denied what was rightfully hers by her very own mother. I hated what this woman had done to my girl, the love of my life, my future wife. I wanted to kill this bitch. It was only when I chased away Scarlet's demons could I get her back. I constantly worked on righting the wrongs that had been done to Scarlet. There was a way I could get her inheritance if I was just diligent and never gave up. Eventually, I won and the check was sent in the mail. That's why My Scarlet called me. I wasn't sure what she wanted. We were done and she would never know what I did for her, but I was fine with that. As long as she was happy, it didn't matter. But she kissed me—took me back. And I was happy; Joyous, stupendous, insane with happiness that I had Scarlet and she was mine. For the first time, she was My Scarlet. *Mine.* I wasn't going to let her go—ever. I can never be tempted with another girl, another life, another cheat because I finally had what other men dream of, a fiancé that is my best friend and my greatest lover. Wait, I haven't gotten to that part yet." I stopped and looked up at him, unsure what he meant. He was smiling at me, with his hand in his pocket. I picked up where I left off. "After we moved in together, I bought the ring, had it custom made, of course, and asked her brother for permission. He gave me his approval with a hug, and I decided to ask her. I wanted to ask her a long time ago, but I wanted to wait, make sure she was ready to commit to me. What if she changed her mind about me? What if she couldn't trust me? What if she didn't love me? I wanted to make love to her, but I wanted her to know it would be the first of the rest of our lives—I wasn't going anywhere. So, I got down on one knee." I stopped and looked up at Sean. He was kneeling on the floor in front of me, smiling as he held the ring out to me.

"Keep going," he said.

I looked back at the book, but my vision was starting to blur from the tears. I found the sentence. "I didn't ask her and she didn't answer. There was no need." That was the last line. I put down the book and looked at him. He still held out the ring to me.

"I'm not going to ask you," he said as he grabbed my hand. He put the ring on my finger and it sparkled in the light. I couldn't believe this was happening and how romantic it was. I knew Sean regretted our past, but he knew the events of our lives only made us stronger as a couple. If we could get through all of that, then we really were meant for each other.

I wiped my tears away. "And I'm not going to answer."

Sean rose to a stand and kissed my tears away. I wrapped my arms around him and held him tightly, letting myself feel the moment of pure joy. Sean held me and said nothing for a while then he kissed me gently.

"That was beautiful, Sean," I whispered. "I'm so happy."

"Not as beautiful as My Scarlet."

I smiled at him. "I like that."

"Good," he said. He turned the ring on my finger, exposing the bottom of the white gold. Engraved in the metal were the words, *My Scarlet*.

Sean stared at me for a moment then grabbed my face and kissed me. His fingers still held my hand that wore the engagement ring, and he played with it while he kissed me. He moved his hands to my neck then ran his fingers through my hair. His hand slid down my chest until he reached the end of my shirt then he pulled it over my head. My heart raced in my chest as I realized that we were finally doing this.

"I think you are ready," he said as he unclasped my bra and let it fell to the floor.

"About time," I said as I unbuttoned his shirt and pulled it from his body.

Sean laughed despite the seriousness of the moment. "You deserve a special moment."

Sean grabbed me in his arms then laid me on the bed. He removed my pants and underwear then removed his own. Soon his naked body was touching mine and I felt my body lose control as he crawled on top of me. The lit candles in the room glowed brightly, and the soft rose petals caressed my skin on the bed. All of that, in addition to his proposal, made the tears fall from my eyes. He kissed them away while he separated my legs with his own.

"I love you," I whispered.

"I love you, too."

I moaned as I felt him move within me. Sean kissed me as he rocked my body, and I felt the tightness in my frame as Sean brought me to climax, where I whispered his name over and over until it passed. Somehow, the lovemaking was even better than last time. I felt connected to him in a way that I never had. Perhaps it was because I knew this was it—the real thing. Sean was completely committed to me in every way. There was no one else. Sean sucked on my bottom lip gently and the touch made me charged all over again. I gripped his back as the feeling of pleasure expanded through me and took complete dominance over my mind. I pressed my forehead against his, and breathed into his mouth as I lost control of my movements. I moaned loudly as he made me explode again.

"You're the best I ever had," I whispered.

"That's because you love me." He breathed deeply near my ear. "And only me." Sean ran his hands through my hair as I massaged his back gently. His body stiffened under my touch and I knew he was meeting his euphoria too. I whispered my love for him into his ear as he came inside me, surrendering his entire soul to me. Sean stared at me until he finished then rested his forehead against mine.

I ran my hands through his hair as I met his gaze. "I'm glad we waited," I said.

Sean kissed me. "Good," he said. "I hope it was everything you wanted it to be."

"It was." I smiled at him. "But I'm not waiting ever again."

Sean laughed. "You can be a total slut now."

"And I will. I want you to fuck my brains out."

"And I will," he said with a smile. "Let's go to Mega-Shake," he said. "Everyone is waiting for us."

"They are?" I said sadly.

"What's wrong?"

I pulled him closer to me. "Let's stay here."

Sean laughed. "We have the rest of our lives."

"Fine," I sighed. "But as soon as we get home, you're mine."

"I expect nothing less," he said as he got up and dressed himself. "I'll make your legs shake, babe."

When I changed my clothes, I looked at the ring on my finger and admired its beauty and shine. The diamonds were sparkling even in the dim lighting of the room. The candles still flickered, and the rose pedals were in disarray from our lovemaking.

"That was so romantic, Sean," I said. "I never took you as a sentimental guy."

"Only for you," he said as he grabbed my hand. "Let's go. Everyone is getting anxious."

We took a cab to the restaurant, and I continued to admire my ring. "It's beautiful," I said.

"I'm glad you like it. Everyone helped me pick it out. It was difficult for all of us to go without your knowledge."

"You needed all of them?" I asked with a laugh.

"Well, they are all your family," he said as he held my hand. "They had the right to be involved."

"So, that's why Cortland took me to lunch?" I said. "So you could get ready?"

"Yes." He smiled.

"You're sneaky."

The cab stopped in front of the restaurant and as soon as we walked inside, everyone jumped and yelled "Surprise!" There was banner across the room that said, CONGRATULATIONS SEAN AND SCARLET. There was no one else in the restaurant and Sean recognized my thought.

"We rented it out," he explained.

Ryan walked over to me and hugged me, lifting me from the ground as he spun me in a circle. "I'm so happy for you," he said. "I love you."

"I love you, too."

Ryan turned to Sean. "Thank you so much," he said as they shook hands.

"For what?" Sean asked.

"Now I don't have to deal with her anymore."

"You are going to tease me during my engagement party?" I snapped.

Sean suddenly looked uncomfortable. "Wait, so I have to deal with *all* of her problems?" he asked hesitantly. "I thought she would still go to you."

Ryan shook his head with smile. "Hell no," he said. "She's your problem now."

Sean turned to me with his palm raised up. "Can I have my ring back?"

I hit him on the shoulder and Sean laughed. "You're stuck with me," I said.

Sean wrapped his arm around me and kissed my head. "I'm okay with that."

I turned to Ryan. "And you are still stuck with me and my

problems. Just because I'm marrying Sean doesn't mean our relationship will change."

Ryan made a sad face. "Damn it," he said.

I hit him on the shoulder then walked away. Janice hugged me next and held me tightly. "I am so happy for you," she said in an excited voice. "It was so hard not to tell you."

"I'm glad you kept it in."

Cortland came to me next and hugged me. "You look happy," he said. "I'm guessing you finally did the deed."

I smiled at him. "Can you tell?"

Cortland laughed. "Congrats, sis," he said.

"You are a much nicer brother than Ryan is," I said.

"It's probably because I haven't had to put up with you as long."

I hit him on the shoulder and walked away. "I hate all of you."

"Let's take a picture," Janice said as she clapped her hands together. She walked over to one of the employees and handed him the camera. We ran back to the booth and stood together, with Sean and I in the middle.

Ryan raised his voice. "On the count of three."

Janice counted down, and on the last number, Ryan yelled. "I don't share milk products!"

I laughed so hard that I covered my face and bent over. Sean leaned his head back and hit his knee with laughter. Cortland reached for Ryan to give him a high five right when the employee took the picture. Janice just looked dumbfounded.

"You ruined the picture, Ryan!" I yelled.

"I think he made it perfect," Sean said as he smiled at me. He grabbed my face and kissed me. Everyone around us made disgusted faces when we kissed, and then the employee took another picture.

"Let's actually take a good picture," Janice said as she glared at us.

"Fine," Ryan said. We all huddled together with smiles on our faces until the camera light went off and the picture was taken.

"Now was that so hard?" Janice laughed.

"You don't know my brother very well," I teased.

"That's probably why we're still together," Janice said.

Ryan walked over to her and kissed her hard on the mouth. She melted at his touch, and ran her hands through his hair. He pulled away and smiled at her. "*That's* why we are still together."

Sean and I gave them a disgusted look then sat in our booth. The employees brought our burgers and fries over, but when the worker handed me mine, he dropped it on the ground. "I'm so sorry," he said. "I'll bring you another one."

"Don't worry about it," Ryan said quickly.

I picked up the burger and took a bite out of it. "It's fine," I said.

Sean stared at me with a look of disgust. He handed me his milkshake. "Do you want to try mine?"

"That's gross," I said as I took another bite of my burger.

"It's not too late," Cortland said to Sean. "Get out now while you can."

Sean grabbed my face and kissed me even though I was chewing my food. "You are lucky you are such a hot piece of ass."

"So, you would kiss any hot girl who ate their food off the ground?"

"No." He smiled. "Only you."

The story

continues....

Edge of Love

(Book Three in the Forever and Always Series)

Available Now

About the Author

E. L. Todd was raised in California where she attended California State University, Stanislaus and received her bachelor's degree in biological sciences, then continued onto her master's degree in education. While she considers science to be interesting, her true passion is writing. *Forever and Always* is the second installment of the *Forever and Always Series.* She is also the author of the *Soul Saga Trilogy* and an assistant editor at Final-Edits.com.

By E. L. Todd

Soul Catcher

(Book One of the Soul Saga)

Only For You

(Book One of the Forever and Always Series)

Forever and Always

(Book Two of the Forever and Always Series)

Edge of Love

(Book Three of the Forever and Always Series)

Soul Binder

(Book Two of the Soul Saga)

(Available December 2013)

Printed in Great Britain
by Amazon